I0778396

The Dating Drama

1

———

The last time I saw my boyfriend was on a gigantic digital billboard prominently displayed in the middle of Gangnam, Seoul. Funny how I saw him more in advertisements than in real life—but that's just the way it is when you're dating a celebrity. His hectic filming and promo schedule were to blame. But today was the day we would finally see each other again.

Sweet daydreams filled my head as I floated in a haze of bliss towards the reunion with my love. Nothing could spoil my good mood. Absolutely nothing.

I skipped and twirled along the route to Shin Jinseung's apartment building, headphones blasting feel-good K-pop in my ears. In my daydreamy state, I stepped out onto the street to cross the road, oblivious to the fact that the pedestrian signal had turned red. A screech of car brakes followed, then the long, loud honk of a horn. The irate driver rolled down his window and yelled at me. "Oi! Watch where you're going, *oeguk saram!*"

"Oops. Sorry," I said sheepishly. I brushed the incident off and continued on my way. *Nice try, but you can't ruin my mood that easily.*

The gleaming tower of luxury residential apartments where Jinseung lived entered my view, and I hurried my pace, winding through the crowded footpath. When I reached the main entrance, I reminded myself that it was safer to slip in through one of the hidden side doors. After four months as a couple, we were still keeping our relationship a secret, and I couldn't enter and leave his apartment building willy nilly lest we get caught.

I took a roundabout path to the other side of the building, carefully surveying my surroundings, checking no one was watching me. When the coast was clear, I entered a nondescript door marked "no entry" with a swipe of my key card—Jinseung had gifted me his spare one.

The door led into a narrow, windowless corridor which eventually opened out to the elevators in the lobby. From there, I made my way to the twentieth floor.

Butterflies in my stomach, I quickly checked my appearance in my compact mirror. Jinseung was around gorgeous actors and models all the time, so I had to look my best. After touching up my lipstick, I took a deep breath and told myself not to worry. *You've got this. He's not interested in anyone except you.* The relationship was doomed if I allowed myself to be the victim of poor self-esteem.

I took a calming breath before pressing my finger to the doorbell. Jinseung opened the door immediately. You would think I'd be used to his amazing good looks by now, but my jaw still dropped at the sight of him. In fact, he looked even better than I remembered. His bright, smiley eyes scanned me while he bit his lip, and his lean, toned body dressed in a slim-fitting black t-shirt and jeans leaned up against the door frame, arms folded. I felt myself falling for him all over again.

"What are you standing around for?" Jinseung asked with a charming smirk. "Come in."

I shook myself out of my lovestruck stupor and followed him inside. He turned on some music—a quirky acoustic love song which suited my mood.

"Would you like something to drink?" he asked, walking towards the kitchen.

"Sure. What have you got?"

He held up an expensive-looking bottle of wine. "Would this lovely little bottle of exquisite French wine suffice, my lady?"

"That will do nicely."

He poured two glasses then beckoned me to sit down with him on the black leather couch. "God, I've missed you," he said. "It feels like forever since I last saw you."

"I've missed you too. Dating you feels like I'm still single half the time," I admitted.

"Thank you for being so patient."

"Even for the small snatches of time we get to spend together, it's worth it."

"I'm glad you think so. Still, you put up with a lot to be with me. I'm well aware of that. Not everyone would do it."

I shrugged. "It's all part of the package of dating someone famous. How is your schedule looking now, anyway?"

"You'll be pleased to know that I've finished all my scenes for Love's Awakening. Apart from a couple auditions coming up, I'm a free man."

"That's a relief." An invisible weight lifted from my shoulders. I could have him all to myself—at least for a little while. I recalled the promise he made to me six months ago—we would go public with our relationship in one year. We had already made it half-way through. If I could just hold on for six more months, we wouldn't have to sneak around anymore. I couldn't wait.

Jinseung took a sip of his wine. "How's teaching going? Are the kids still keeping you on your toes?"

"Well, they've finally stopped asking me questions about my time on Hidden History, but I still wish they'd focus more."

"I'd be distracted too, if you were my teacher." He sidled up to me, a mischievous look on his face. "It's been so long I've forgotten what it's like to kiss you. Help me remember?"

I grimaced at his corny line but still found him irresistible. I leaned in to kiss him, but stopped short to observe the cute, slightly ridiculous look on his face—his eyes closed tight and lips puckered in anticipation. I couldn't help but giggle.

He opened his eyes. "What? You tease." He pulled me to him with an aggression that thrilled me. His lips found mine, hot and sweet. He wasted no time in deepening the kiss, tongue exploring my mouth with fervour. His body pressed up against mine. I had to pull away for breath. He turned his attention to kissing my neck before returning to my lips and pulling me into his lap. I squirmed to get into a comfortable position, but ended up kicking my wine glass over and spilling it on the floor. I turned my head to check the damage.

"It doesn't matter," Jinseung mumbled, fumbling with my buttons.

I returned my focus to him, settling in his lap, feeling his body rub up against me. He was in the process of pushing me down onto my back when another disruption arose—the doorbell. "Ignore it," he implored.

"But—"

"Please."

"Who could that be? What if they're waiting outside? What if they can *hear* us?"

"It's probably just Changsoo. No one else can get up here anyway, except the cleaner."

"He might let himself in if you don't answer. He knows your door code, right?"

"Ugh. You're right."

Changsoo knew about our relationship, but it would still be awkward if he barged in on us during such a private moment.

We quickly untangled ourselves, tidied our outfits and hair. Jinseung went to the door. He peered through the hole to check who was there. "Huh? They've gone."

"That's weird."

He opened the door and glanced around the corridor. "No one's here. Oh—" Something caught his attention. He bent down and reemerged holding a cardboard box.

"What's that?" I asked.

"I don't know. It was outside the door."

"Not expecting any deliveries?"

"I don't get packages here. They come to my private post box or to the agency."

"Ah. Does it say anything?"

"Nope. No label or anything."

"Could a fan have put it there?"

"I hope not. So far I've managed to avoid fans finding out my home address."

"Are you going to open it?"

"Yeah. Maybe I'll be able to find out who it's from and how it got here."

He brought the package to the dining table where he opened it with a knife. He peered inside the box, rummaged a little, then suddenly recoiled with a look of distaste.

"What? What is it?" I asked.

"It's…nothing. Never mind." He closed the box.

"I can tell that it's not nothing. Let me see."

"I'd rather you didn't."

"Don't hide things from me."

Jinseung reluctantly stood aside and let me open the box. Heart pounding in my chest, I pulled one cardboard flap open, and then the other. What I saw made a shriek escape my throat. There, lying atop a pile of shredded paper, was a mutilated Barbie doll—its limbs twisted and disfigured. Its eyes stabbed out. Its plastic body stained red. *Human blood?!*

"What the heck! Who would send you something like that?"

"Probably a *sasaeng* fan or something. Don't worry about it. Stuff like this happens all the time when you're famous. Occupational hazard." He closed the box again and put it by the rubbish bin.

"How can you take this so lightly? This *sasaeng* fan must know where you live!" I knew all about *sasaeng* fans and the crazy stuff they were capable of—extreme stalking, letters written in blood, breaking into a celebrity's house in their underwear, poisoning their idol's drinks, to name a few.

Jinseung chewed this over. "You're right. That does present a problem. I'll let the security team know tomorrow."

"Tomorrow? But this crazy person could still be in the building this very moment! You should call the police."

He shook his head. "That would be a vast overreaction. If I called the police every time a fan did something disturbing, there'd be no end to it."

I sighed helplessly. "I suppose you're right."

"Please don't let it worry you. I've had fans do weird shit in the past and it's never amounted to anything. Come on." He led me back to the couch and placed a comforting arm around me. "Everything will be okay."

"Well, if you're sure…"

"Absolutely." He massaged my shoulders, trying to put me at ease.

My tension began to dissolve. Celebrities dealt with stuff like this every day. Besides, the security in this building was top-class. They would be able to catch the culprit through checking the CCTV footage as soon as Jinseung told them what happened.

He turned my head towards his and kissed me again, tenderly stroking my cheek. I tried to get into it but couldn't. My thoughts kept turning back to the doll. The image of the blonde-haired, blue-eyed, blood-stained toy seared in my mind. A frightening idea began to take form, and I broke away from the kiss with a gasp.

"What's wrong?" Jinseung asked, concern flashing in his eyes.

"The doll..." I croaked. "What if it represents me?"

2

Silence reigned as twenty-five faces stared up at me with blank expressions. I repeated my question and not a single person raised their hand to answer.

Teaching at the *hagwon* was like speaking into a void a lot of the time. I found it difficult to get the kids to engage with me. They all just sat silently with their exercise books open in front of them, happy to listen but unwilling to say a word, or even to express a grain of interest. At first, I didn't mind this behaviour, but as the months wore on, it began to frustrate me. *Perhaps I'm not cut out to be a teacher.*

The only thing which seemed to excite my students was the fact that I used to star in a K-drama with Shin Jinseung and Baek Yena, but by now we had thoroughly exhausted that topic.

I clicked through to the next slide in my presentation on the large LED screen adjacent to the whiteboard at the back of the classroom. The topic was "text language" and common acronyms used in online forums, which I thought was a fun topic for teenagers. but before I could begin, a short bell ring signalled the end of the lesson, and the students quickly dispersed.

During the five-minute break between classes, I checked my phone, hoping for an update from Jinseung regarding the doll incident, but there were no new messages. Jinseung had convinced me that the doll didn't represent me—it was just the most common kind of doll available to buy. Still, I had hoped for some progress regarding identifying the culprit. Jinseung said he would speak to the building staff, but I didn't know the outcome. Before I had time to type a message, the next batch of students began to filter into the room. My eye was drawn to a new student in the group. She was tall, with long hair pulled back in a high ponytail. Thick-framed glasses gave her a studious look, along with the over-stuffed leather satchel on her hip and the large ring binder hugged to her chest. She was wearing a school uniform I hadn't seen before—a cream-coloured sweater over a white shirt with a neat bow tied below the collar. On the bottom, a red-plaid pleated skirt and white over-the-knee socks. I wondered which high school she went to.

When everyone had settled down in the bright orange ergonomic chairs behind their desks, I asked the new student to introduce herself. To my surprise, she got up and stood in front of the class. "My name is Kim Sungmi," she said. "I am eighteen years old. I am joining your class from now on." Her voice was quiet but assured. She spoke English well.

"Thank you, Kim Sungmi."

As was tradition, I asked her to pick an English name for her to use in the class. She picked Sophie.

When Sophie had returned to her seat, I put up my slides for the day's lesson. We would be going over some common homonyms, and I had prepared a little game. The slides displayed multiple sentences, but only one sentence on each was correct. I tasked the class with telling me which were right, and even threw in a bribe of candy.

At the beginning of the first round of the game, I was fully prepared to be met by bored expressions as usual, but to my surprise, a hand shot up. It was Sophie.

"Yes, Sophie?"

"Number three," she said.

I clicked to the next screen and a red tick mark animation appeared beside the third sentence. "That's correct. Well done." I put a small wrapped candy on her desk.

Sophie answered correctly twice more, and then something unexpected happened—another couple of tentative hands rose into the air. And after a few more rounds, other members of the class started to join in. Sophie's enthusiasm seemed to be contagious.

After the game, keeping the class engaged was a breeze. The entire lesson flew by, and before I knew it, class was over. The classroom slowly emptied until the only student who remained was Sophie. She approached my desk. "Excuse me, Ms. Gibson."

"How can I help you?" I asked, a little taken aback. No one had stayed behind to talk to me before.

Sophie blushed. "I was wondering if you could recommend some English books to read."

"Of course. What kind of books?"

"Novels. But ones that are simple to read."

"What is your English level?"

"Around B2."

I opened my notebook and compiled a short list of titles, before tearing out the page and passing it to her. She accepted it eagerly.

"And if you can't find any of these, I'd be happy to bring some books from home for you to borrow."

"Thank you," Sophie said, glowing with gratitude. She carefully folded and stowed the piece of notepaper in the front pocket of her satchel.

"Have a good evening," I said.

"Good evening." She bowed.

What a breath of fresh air, I thought, watching her leave the classroom.

———

Drip. Drip. Drip. Streetlamps illuminated clusters of raindrops in the darkness.

I had just left work. Like most *hagwons*—a.k.a cram schools, students attended in the late afternoon or in the evening. My teaching hours were four through nine, but normally I arrived earlier to prepare, and left later to mark student work. On this night, I had stayed around an hour late.

I opened my umbrella—a cheap transparent one, and set out at a quick pace, dashing through puddles which splashed up my ankles. The bus was already at the stop, route number 76 displayed on its back in orange digits.

I ran as fast as I could, but the bus started to indicate, and it pulled out into the flow of traffic before I could reach it. I sagged in defeat, puffing.

After I had caught my breath, I checked the schedule affixed to the back of the glass bus shelter. To my dismay, the next bus wouldn't be for another forty minutes. I made up my mind to walk home rather than wait, hopeful that the rain wouldn't intensify.

Normally I stuck to main streets as much as I could whenever I walked home from work, but in my desperation to get back as quickly as possible, I decided to take a shortcut.

The steep, narrow side street had no footpath and cars were parked haphazardly along one side. I carefully made my way down the road, avoiding slippery smooth parts. As I walked, my ears pricked at the sound of footsteps following me. Panic surged through my body—I was still on edge after the doll incident. I turned around just to check who was there and put my mind at ease. All was still and quiet on the empty street, not a soul in sight. I shrugged and moved on. *It must have been my imagination.*

A few steps later, I heard the sound again. Without pausing to think, I turned my head. I caught sight of a figure, but before I could process anything about the person, they had entered a shop and disappeared, the door swinging shut with a bang behind them. I was alone on the quiet road again. I admonished myself for being so paranoid.

3

———

"Ewww, that's disgusting!" Yang Bora said, face screwed up in revulsion.

I had just finished relaying a graphic description of the mutilated, bloodstained Barbie doll delivery. We were in the kitchen of my apartment, getting food and drinks ready for an afternoon binge-watching K-dramas.

"Do you think a *sasaeng* fan could have done it?" I asked, turning the electric kettle on to make tea.

Recovering from her initial disgust, Bora adjusted her circle-framed glasses. "Sounds like the work of a *sasaeng* fan, all right. Though what could be their motivation? A warning perhaps. Don't date anyone?"

"I was afraid that the doll might represent me."

Bora shuddered. "Now that's a scary theory. I truly hope that's not the case. Has the culprit been ascertained?"

I shook my head. "They were caught on the security cameras bribing the concierge to find out Jinseung's apartment number. Unfortunately, they were wearing a black motorcycle helmet and dark clothing. Don't even know if it was a man or a woman."

"So they could still be at large…Has anything else happened since then?"

"No. Nothing." Except a strange feeling that I was being followed, but I had no concrete evidence and put that firmly down to paranoia.

"Well, I'm sure that concierge was sacked, and no one will be let up to Jinseung's apartment again."

"Yeah. No doubt."

"And if something like this happens again, KAM will definitely up the ante on his personal security. So I wouldn't worry too much if I were you."

"You're right. Though I feel I should be careful."

"You should always be careful anyway—dating someone so high-profile." She sighed. "After all this, I think we should watch something nice and comforting."

"I couldn't agree more. How about a family drama?"

"Good idea."

I prepared a pot of English breakfast tea and opened the seven-eleven shopping bag Bora had brought over with her. "Nice selection," I said, examining the variety of colourfully packaged treats inside. I arranged them on the bench.

"I know you're addicted to those honey butter chips."

"They're my absolute favourite. Thank you."

We relocated to the lounge—a nook in the open-plan living area containing a small cream-coloured sectional topped with a mountain of soft cushions, and a fluffy faux-fur rug at our feet. I laid out the tea and snacks on the coffee table. Bora had already gained control of the TV remote and proceeded to browse the catalogue of shows on the large screen opposite us.

Meeting regularly to binge-watch K-dramas and chat had

become a regular activity for me and Bora, vastly favoured over going out to restaurants and bars, plus more frugal as well. I was so happy that we had managed to maintain our friendship despite our busy schedules. She hadn't changed a bit since we worked together—apart from the more sophisticated wardrobe and designer handbag she had procured after her promotion.

After some deliberation, we picked Ojakgyo Family, which seemed to fit the bill of a warm and cosy family drama. Neither of us had watched it before.

"Joo Won is so hot," Bora said with a wistful sigh, sinking lower onto the couch. "I suppose you can't relate to celebrity crushes anymore. You're already dating one."

I hit her lightly with a cushion. "I still think Joo Won is hot. Don't tell Jinseung."

Joo Won aside, as I watched the episode, I couldn't help but think about my time on Hidden History and the amazing experience of being part of a K-drama. A surge of longing flowed through my veins, a melancholy feeling that I'd never get to experience that same thrill again.

"I miss it…" I murmured.

"What?"

"Acting. Being in Hidden History was the best time of my life. And not just because I met Shin Jinseung."

"I get that. Teaching must feel boring in comparison."

"It does."

Bora nudged me playfully. "Why don't you get back into entertainment?"

I shook her off. "It's too difficult as a foreigner."

"There's gotta be something else out there for you."

"I'm not that optimistic. No. I think I'll stick to teaching. It's solid work. It pays the bills."

She rolled her eyes. "Solid work that pays the bills...so boring."

"There's one good thing. A new girl started recently, and she's been making teaching worthwhile for me. Her name's Kim Sungmi."

"Sounds like you've found your star student."

"Yes. I think so too."

We returned our attention to the episode and refilled our mugs with tea.

"Uee is funny looking, isn't she? But still pretty." Bora assessed the female lead, nibbling on a bar of Ghana milk chocolate.

Partway through the third consecutive episode, her phone began to ring in a tone which got progressively louder until she fished it out of the depths of her handbag.

She grimaced as she looked at who was calling her. "Can you pause it? I need to take this. It's Go Yoojin."

"Sure."

Go Yoojin was the teenage actor Bora was managing. She had a reputation for being a major drama queen, and Bora had confirmed this to me on a number of occasions.

Bora answered the call. Go Yoojin spoke in a shrill, high-pitched voice which I could hear despite my distance from the phone. She seemed to be having some kind of a crisis.

"Stay calm," Bora told her. "I'll be there in a minute." She ended the phone call. "I've got to go. Yoojin's having another one of her little meltdowns. On my day off too. Ugh. Sorry, Chloe."

"No problem. Hope she's okay."

"It's probably something trivial. Last time she called me like this it was because she couldn't find her favourite top."

"I'm sure she's grateful to have you to rely on."

"Yeah, I guess. Anyway, I better get going." She grabbed her leather jacket and put it on. "Don't watch any more episodes without me, okay? I'll try to come back later."

"Okay, buh-bye."

The door shut behind her with a click.

I put the remaining snacks away before they could tempt me, then flung myself in a heap on the couch, wondering what to do for the rest of the afternoon.

My eyes wandered to my diary which lay atop the coffee table. If there were any errands or tasks I needed to get done, they would be listed within its pages. I reached for the leather-covered notebook and opened it to the thin, red ribbon bookmark. Scanning the page, a note I had scribbled down a few days ago caught my eye—*English books for Sophie.* It reminded me to check my bookshelf for something that might interest her.

I ran my fingers along the spines of the titles housed in my bookshelf. I did not have a large collection, since I left most of my books behind in England, and I hadn't procured many new titles since moving to Seoul. Out of the few books I did possess, I pulled out any which looked promising. I settled back on the couch with the small pile of books on my lap and proceeded to read a few pages of each to determine whether they would be appropriate for someone still learning the language.

After deciding the first book was too difficult, I started a stack of rejects on the coffee table. As I checked each book, the reject stack grew. I held out hope for the last book in my hands, but quickly realised that it too would be inappropriate. I put the books back on the shelf, annoyed that my chance to do something nice for a student had been dashed. *Or had it?* A new idea popped into my head. There was a bookshop not too far from my place and it stocked a few English books. I had nothing else to do that afternoon, so why not go and have a browse? Besides, I was short on reading material, and if I ended up buying something for Sophie to borrow, I could read it after her.

Before leaving my apartment, I put on a woollen hat and scarf—it was early spring, but the weather was still wintery. I decided to walk to the bookshop rather than taking the subway, pushing my recent paranoia about being followed to the back of my mind. I needed the exercise, and I hadn't been outside all day, so the fresh, crisp air was welcome—despite the hint of pollution.

The brisk walk quickly warmed me up, especially as there were a lot of steep roads to climb. After winding through the network of narrow backstreets dense with houses, convenience stores, and small restaurants, I emerged in a busy shopping area. The bookshop was located between a chain coffee shop and a pharmacy. "Ginger Books," read the sign above a large window peering into the warm and cosy interior.

I removed my hat and scarf upon entering the shop and tucked them away in my bag. Like most indoor spaces in Seoul during cold weather, the shop was well-heated, necessitating the removal of layers.

Tall shelving units formed aisles with display tables around the border. A few patrons quietly browsed. I headed straight for the English-language section. Running my eyes over the shelves, I realised there were fewer books than I had hoped. I examined them one by one, looking for something easy to read, but with subject matter appealing enough for someone in their late teens.

As I spent my time perusing, I felt the eyes of the shop

assistant behind the counter watching me. I suspected that he wasn't used to seeing foreigners in the shop. I simply ignored him and continued with my task.

After a thorough assessment of all the titles, I ended up selecting three and took them to the counter. The shop assistant continued to stare at me even as we were face to face during the transaction. His brow was furrowed slightly. He looked like he was trying to place me.

"Do we know each other?" I ventured.

He looked at me with surprise, possibly at my ability to speak Korean, and he averted his gaze as if suddenly embarrassed by his behaviour. "Maybe," he said. "I'm sure I've seen you somewhere before."

I looked him up and down. "I'm sorry. I don't recognise you."

"Is that so?" He hummed as the receipt printed out. He slipped it inside the cover of one of the books, then placed them in a plastic bag emblazoned with the store's logo—a curled-up ginger cat.

I put away my wallet and grabbed the bag.

The shop assistant snapped his fingers. "Ah! I've seen you on television. You were in that drama."

So that's what he recognised me from. I was surprised. It had been several months since the drama aired and no one had recognised me since. "Yes. I was in Hidden History."

"That's the one!"

"Well, I'll be going now…"

"Wait! Can I take a picture? I like to show the other staff members whenever someone famous visits the store."

I scoffed slightly. "I'm not famous."

"Please. My colleague was obsessed with that drama."

"Oh, all right then."

He whipped out his phone and took a couple of photos.

I relaxed again when the phone was back in his pocket.

"Thanks," he said. "Enjoy the books."

I departed the bookshop feeling slightly perturbed. I thought my days of being recognised were behind me, but it appeared I was mistaken.

4

I hadn't been expecting to see the mangled doll again, yet there it was, exactly where Jinseung had left it the last time I visited his apartment—in the cardboard box next to the rubbish bin.

I had almost tripped over the box on my way out of the kitchen, then jumped back in fright, catching a glimpse of the creepy doll under the flimsy cardboard flap. Shuddering, I hurried away to confront Jinseung. "You didn't get rid of the doll?" I asked, aghast.

He sat on the couch, hunched over playing a video game on the TV. He put the controller down and rubbed the back of his neck sheepishly. "Oh that. I haven't gotten around to it. Changsoo said I should keep it as evidence, in case something like this happens again and I need proof, but I can't bring myself to go near it…to touch it…I've just been ignoring it. Helps that I haven't been home that much lately."

"Still, you can't just leave it there! How can you even live with that thing right there!"

"I know. Perhaps I should tackle the job now."

My gut clenched. I'd feel better if he got rid of the doll, but I didn't want to watch. "You should. I won't be able to think of anything else knowing that it's still sitting in that box, right where you left it before."

"Then I'll do it."

"I don't want to look, though."

"Close your eyes."

"That's not enough to detract my attention from what you're doing."

"Shut yourself in the bedroom while I take care of it then."

"Now?" I hummed in consideration. "Okay. Come and get me when you're done."

I crossed the living room to his bedroom and closed myself inside. I sat on the end of his bed while I waited. The process seemed to be taking some time, so I lay back and stared up at the ceiling, trying not to think about it.

Jinseung opened the door a few minutes later. He seemed flustered, his ears and cheeks tinted bright pink. "It's taken care of."

I snapped upright. "What did you do with it?"

"I wore rubber gloves and put it in a ziplock bag. I stored it in a drawer for now. Maybe I'll get Changsoo to take it off my hands…"

"Good idea. I'd feel better if it wasn't in this house, but for now, I'll tolerate it."

"I got rid of the box too."

"Good."

Jinseung shuffled on his feet, an anxious look upon his face.

"Is something wrong?" I asked.

He shook his head. "No…it's nothing. Don't worry."

I raised an eyebrow, unconvinced. Before I could press him further, he extended a hand and tugged me off the bed. He drew me into his arms and kissed my forehead.

"I'm sorry this happened," he murmured, lips against my skin.

"It's not your fault."

"You've seen one of the ugly sides of fame now. I should have protected you from it."

"There was nothing you could do."

"I suppose not." He sighed. "Anyway, let's not dwell on that anymore. Come on. I've got a two-player game we can play." His arm around me, he walked me back to the living room.

———

"I win again," Jinseung teased, after beating me what must have been the tenth time in a row.

"Ugh," I grumbled. "I suck at these kinds of games!" I tossed the controller to the side in frustration.

He chuckled. "Perhaps we should take a break. You hungry?"

"Famished."

"Shall we go get something to eat then? There's no food here."

"You mean, should *I* go and get something to eat." It seemed trivial, but one of the things I disliked about dating him was that I always had to be the one to go out and pick up food.

He flashed me a sympathetic look. "I know it's a pain. Sorry. I'll make it up to you later."

I huffed. "Fine. I'll go. That Chinese place you like?"

"Yep. Sounds good."

I called the restaurant to place an order, then got ready to leave a bit later.

"Don't forget to get some of that yummy sauce they have," Jinseung reminded me on my way out the door.

"Got it." I made a mental note.

On my way to the nearby Chinese restaurant, I stuffed my hands in the fleece-lined pockets of my jacket. My breath came out in puffs of mist in the night air. The streets were busy, and I could hear music in the distance. I remembered that there was a lantern festival on at the park. I would have gone if I hadn't made plans to spend the evening with Jinseung. *If only we could go together.* I tried to shrug off my disappointment.

The restaurant looked like nothing special from the outside. An LED sign flickered and buzzed above the door, two of the characters missing due to the bulbs having died. Fragrant ginger, garlic, and cooking oil assailed my nose when I entered. The takeaway area was packed with customers, all the waiting seats were taken up, and a line trailed from the counter. A door on the left led to a dining area with plastic chairs, tables lined with paper tablecloths, and faded posters on the walls. The restaurant was much busier than usual thanks to the festival. All of the tables were full with hungry patrons, the noise of their loud chatter mixing with the clanging and splattering sounds from the kitchen.

I waited in the queue at the counter only to be informed that my order would take at least another ten minutes due to how busy they were. Feeling cramped in the small waiting area, I went outside and sent a message to Jinseung saying I would be a while. I stood leaning with my back against the wall, watching the crowds of people on their way to and from the festival. Many cute couples passed by, holding hands or with their arms around one another. A lot of them were dressed in *hanbok*. A wave of longing washed over me. Would I ever be able to do that with Jinseung in public? Those couples looked so carefree. I couldn't help feeling a pang of jealousy.

After waiting ten minutes, I went back inside. Soon enough, my order was ready. The man behind the counter passed me three large polystyrene takeout containers in a plastic bag. I asked for an extra punnet of the sauce Jinseung liked and threw that in as well.

Bag swinging from my hand, I made my way back to Jinseung's place, walking quickly so the food wouldn't get cold.

"That smells good," Jinseung said as I entered.

"Hopefully it was worth the wait."

He relieved me of the bag and unloaded the containers onto the table. "Why was it so busy?"

"The lantern festival is on tonight. The whole area is busy."

"Ohhh. I didn't realise. I should have made alternate dinner plans."

"Never mind. It didn't take *that* long. Let's eat. I'm starving."

We tucked into the overflowing containers of fried rice, dumplings, and sweet-and-sour pork. Despite how basic the restaurant appeared, the food really was delicious.

As we ate, my mind wandered back to the couples on the street. I imagined how romantic it would be to lay out a blanket and sit under the stars, surrounded by lanterns glowing in the moonlight. There would probably be fireworks as well. I was starting to get a major case of FOMO.

"What ya thinking about?" Jinseung asked, pausing between mouthfuls.

"Oh, nothing really." I gathered some fried rice with my chopsticks.

"Is there anything you want to do tonight? I told you I would make it up to you since you had to go out and get the food."

I wish we could go to the festival. "No. Not particularly." I couldn't help the note of melancholy in my voice.

Jinseung frowned, lines appearing on his forehead. "You want to go to the festival, don't you."

Damn. He's a mind reader. "Yeah, but I know that's not possible."

"You can go if you want. You don't have to stay here with me. I won't be offended if you go."

"But I want to go *with you*. It wouldn't be any fun by myself."

Jinseung smiled, his cheeks dimpling. "That's real sweet. Maybe if I disguised myself enough…"

My heart leapt with hope. "Wait—really?"

His smile slowly faded. "Perhaps not. It's kinda risky."

I returned my attention to my meal, disappointed.

"Unless…" He toyed with his chopsticks. "There will be fireworks, won't there?"

"I think so."

"I have an idea."

"What is it?"

"I'm not one hundred per cent sure if this will work, but I'll give it a shot."

I had no idea what he was talking about, but it sounded promising.

"I'll have to go and ask someone," he explained. "So, let's finish eating first."

My curiosity was well and truly piqued, but he wouldn't answer any of my questions, telling me to wait and see.

He slipped out of the apartment after dinner. Several minutes later, he returned, a triumphant look on his face.

"Well?" I asked.

"I just need to grab a few things, then we'll go."

"Go where?"

He didn't answer me. Instead, he disappeared into his room and re-emerged with a backpack slung over his shoulder. Then he went to the kitchen and filled a thermos with boiling water and grabbed something from the pantry. I watched him, bemused.

"Come on," Jinseung beckoned. "Bring your jacket."

Were we going to the festival? How was it possible?

Confusion reigned when Jinseung took me to the stairs rather than the elevator. "Aren't the elevators working?" I asked.

"We can only get to the top floor by the stairs."

"The top floor? Why are we going there?"

"You'll see."

Fortunately, there weren't too many flights of stairs to ascend since Jinseung's apartment was situated on one of the higher floors. At the very end of the staircase, there was a door which read "no entry." I realised that it led to the rooftop, and I understood Jinseung's plan. From the roof, we would be able to see the park and watch the fireworks. Too bad it didn't look like we'd be able to go through the door. I tried the handle, but as expected, it didn't relinquish. "It's locked," I said, frowning.

"Lucky I have the key then, isn't it?" He produced a green lanyard with a key attached from his pocket.

"How did you get that?"

"Had to work my charm on the building staff. Probably

felt they owed me a favour too, since they let that crazy doll person up to my apartment. Anyway, I have the key for the night. I'll return it tomorrow morning." He unlocked the door, and we stepped out onto the rooftop.

I gazed around, absorbing my surroundings. The rooftop was utilitarian—ventilation units, aerials, and satellites on a concrete surface. However, the view was incredible. I leaned up against the fence and peered out over the city, Seoul in all its metropolitan glory—a dazzling array of multicolour lights, sprawling towers, bumper-to-bumper traffic, and thronging pedestrians.

"We're so high up…" I mused, feeling a little dizzy.

"Not scared of heights, are you?" Jinseung asked, standing beside me.

"I'm okay as long as I don't look straight down for too long."

"I know what you mean. It's a big drop."

"Where's the park?"

"Let's see…We're facing east right now, so the park should be somewhere over there." He gestured to his right. "Ah, I see it. Can you?"

I followed his gaze to a large patch of green, swarming with tiny people. The lanterns were reduced to glowing dots, but the sight was still magical.

Jinseung took off his backpack and opened it. He pulled out a blanket and lay it on the ground. He sat down and patted the space beside him. The fence around the perimeter of the rooftop was transparent, so we could still see well from our new viewpoint. I lay on my back and looked up at the sky. It was washed out due to the light pollution, but if I squinted enough, I could make out the stars.

"Want a coffee?" Jinseung asked. He procured the thermos from his backpack and a handful of flavoured coffee sachets.

"Yes, please."

He prepared me a cup and handed it to me. "So, what do you think? I know it's not as good as being at the festival for real…"

I shook my head. "It's perfect."

He smirked. "You're just saying that."

"No, truly. I've never been up on a rooftop so high like this before. It's pretty special."

"I'm glad you think so. Come 'ere." He lifted his arm, beckoning me to snuggle up to him. "Comfy?" he asked when I had wedged myself by his side, his arm around me.

"Very."

"Are you cold?"

"I'm fine. The coffee was a good idea." I cradled the warm cup in my hands.

Jinseung stroked his hand up and down my arm. "I feel kinda bad…not being able to take you to the places you want to see…do the things you want to do. I'm a bad boyfriend. I know it."

"You're not," I argued unconvincingly.

"You don't have to lie to me. It can't be fun being in your position. Sometimes I think you're too patient for your own good. Making sacrifices and compromising…those things aren't my strong point."

"Your ambition is part of what makes you so attractive to me." That was the truth. His work ethic was something I looked up to. Something I wanted to emulate. Just being around him was energising. "I wish I could be more like you."

"Ha! Why would you want to? You have plenty of attractive qualities, yourself."

"Such as?" I sidled up to him, fishing for compliments.

"You're so smart and courageous, coming here and

learning the language when you were so young. You're talented, acting in a drama without any training and doing an excellent job at it. You're beautiful without much effort. You're kind and caring and intelligent. Oh, and I can't forget how fiercely independent you are. You never try to take advantage of my fame or my money, preferring to work things out on your own. I strongly believe that you could achieve anything if you set your mind to it. You just haven't decided what you want to do yet."

His words made me feel all warm and mushy. "You flatter me."

"You deserve all the praise you get."

I threw my arms around him, overwhelmed by his sweet compliments.

We spent the next hour talking about our hopes and dreams, our worries and our fears. It was the most he had ever opened up to me. This whole side of him was most endearing. The invisible barriers between us broke down. We were no longer a famous star and an ordinary young woman, we were simply two humans, sitting side by side on the rooftop.

Jinseung looked so dreamy, the moonlight caressing his skin, illuminating his features in a soft blue tone. His bright eyes sparkled as they looked down at me, full, soft lips quirking at the corner as he noticed me stare. He brushed my cheek with his thumb before catching my lips with his. He kissed me tenderly, but thoroughly, fingers laced in my hair. A soft whimper escaped my mouth when he broke away, and three words came tumbling out before I could help it. "I love you."

Jinseung's forehead wrinkled, an inscrutable expression on his face. He looked into my eyes but didn't say anything.

My cheeks were beginning to burn. *Perhaps I shouldn't have said anything...* A loud screech pierced the air followed by a crackling sound, drawing my attention. Fireworks burst in the sky, shooting colourful sparks through the air.

5

I had a feeling I was forgetting something as I left for work
the next afternoon. Halfway to the bus stop, I froze in my
tracks, realising what it was. The books I had purchased to
lend Sophie were still at home, and it wasn't the first day I
had forgotten to bring them with me. Fortunately, I had
enough time to turn back if I walked quickly.

Dodging the pedestrians in my way, I made it back to my
apartment and grabbed the plastic bag with the ginger cat
logo containing the books. I returned to the bus stop in the
nick of time.

I rode the bus with the bag resting safely on my lap,
thinking how happy Sophie would be to receive the
books. Lending them to her was important to me. Until she
joined my class, teaching was an uninspiring task. Thanks to
her, I was beginning to engage more with the subject and the
students. This little favour was my way of thanking her.

The books sat on my desk until my last class of the day,
when Sophie and the other final-year high school students
took their seats in the room.

As she always did, Sophie emptied the contents of her satchel and arranged the items tidily on her desk. I walked around the classroom handing out homework I had marked. When I reached Sophie, I asked if I could speak with her after class. "I have some books for you," I explained.

"Okay," she said, looking pleased.

Once everyone had left at the end of class, I placed the books on Sophie's desk. "I know that you were struggling to find English books to read. I found these and wanted to lend them to you."

Sophie eagerly picked up one of the books and turned it over in her hands, scanning the blurb. "This is wonderful. Thank you so much."

"I wasn't sure what kind of books you usually read. I hope you enjoy them."

"I'm sure I will!"

"You can borrow them for as long as you need, and if you have any questions, let me know."

"Thank you."

"Are you in a hurry to get home?"

"Not really."

I pulled out the chair from the desk beside hers and sat down. "I wanted to ask you how you're getting on, being new to the class and all."

"Oh. Everything is fine. I'm enjoying it."

"Your English is good."

She blushed. "Thanks."

We had mainly been speaking in English. She only reverted to Korean every now and then when she didn't know how to say something. Compared to most other students her age, she was advanced in her skill.

"I never did ask you what school you're from," I said. "I haven't seen that uniform before."

"Horim High School."

"Never heard of it."

"You wouldn't. It's a small school."

"What subjects are you taking?"

She thought for a moment. "There are a lot. Korean, English, Japanese…history, mathematics, science…technology. There are more."

"Gosh. You have a lot on your plate."

"On your plate?" She crinkled her brow.

"It's an expression," I explained. "It means you're very busy."

"I see." She jotted the phrase down in her notebook, filing it for later.

"Are you taking any other *hagwon* classes besides English?" I enquired.

"No. Just English. It's my most important subject since I want to go to university overseas."

"Oh? Which country?"

"You're from England, aren't you?"

"Yes."

"I'd like to study there if possible. If I can get into a good university."

"I can tell you a lot about universities in England, if that's useful."

"Really? That would be so helpful!"

"It's no problem. We can talk about it another day."

"I look forward to it." She beamed.

"Anyway, I'll let you get home now."

"Thanks for the books!"

"You're welcome."

She stowed them in her satchel. "See you tomorrow."

As Sophie left the classroom, I glowed with the happy

feeling of doing something nice for someone. I resolved to try harder with my other students as well.

I didn't have anything else I needed to get done that evening, so I packed my briefcase and headed out. I was on the bus when a call came from Jinseung.

"Hey, Chloe. Are you free?" His voice sounded strange. "There's something I need to tell you. Can you meet me at Cinema Lumiere?"

"When?"

"As soon as possible."

"What's this about?"

"I'd better tell you in person. I'll see you at the cinema."

He hung up before I could say anything else.

———

Making my way through the fluorescent-lit subway station, something caught my eye and stopped me in my tracks. An entertainment news bulletin played on a small TV above the waiting area. A montage of Shin Jinseung photographs and video clips graced the screen with the words "breaking news" in large red characters.

I moved in closer, determined to find out what it was about, but I had just caught the tail end and the sound was muted. The next item started to play before I could decipher anything.

I wondered if the news story was connected with what Jinseung wanted to tell me. Automatically, I pulled out my phone and started typing "Shin Jinseung news" into the search bar, then rapidly backspaced. *I should give him the chance to tell me himself*, I decided.

I hopped on the next train, rode three stops, and emerged

from the station on a busy six-lane street buzzing with late-night activity.

Through a maze of dark little backstreets, I arrived at Cinema Lumiere, the tiny boutique movie theatre that had become the de facto meeting place for me and Jinseung. His sister worked there and would let us come in after closing, or other times Jinseung would book the entire theatre for a private date.

I announced my arrival via the intercom. The door unlocked. The warm foyer smelled of buttery popcorn. Shin Jina stood wiping down the bar with a yellow cloth. Jinseung didn't seem to have arrived yet.

"Chloeeee!" Jina rushed towards me to give me a hug. "So good to see you. Feels like ages since you last came here." She looked gorgeous as usual, wearing a crisp white shirt over black skinny jeans, hoop earrings, and her hair in a cute pixie cut.

"It has been ages," I replied.

"You should visit even when you're not meeting *Dongsaeng*. I've missed you."

"Then I'll come and watch a movie." I picked up a printed schedule from the bar.

"I'll even let you in for free."

"Really?"

"Of course. Giving my friends free tickets is a perk of the job. I'm going to make myself a coffee. Want anything?"

"Oh, a hot chocolate, please."

"Coming right up." She prepared the hot drinks, tinkering away with the espresso machine.

I pulled up my sleeve and checked my watch. *Jinseung must be running late.* My mind wandered back to the news bulletin. *What could the news possibly be?* Temptation rose in me. *How simple it would be just to do a quick search…*

"Here you go." Jina passed me a mug.

Does Jina know? It doesn't look like she's holding anything back from me.

Determined not to give in to the temptation, I left my phone in my bag, not even allowing myself a quick glance.

Jina and I chatted at the bar, cradling our mugs in our hands, helping me take my mind off Jinseung and whatever it was he had to tell me.

Twenty minutes later, the intercom buzzed. Jina unlocked the door, and Jinseung came in at the same time as a large gust of wind. He looked tired and dishevelled, but still wore a warm smile. "Hey," he said. "Sorry I'm late. Hard to get away. It's been crazy."

"Something to drink?" Jina asked.

He shook his head. "I can't stay long."

He ushered me to a couch below a wall of black-and-white portraits of famous directors.

"You look exhausted," I said, looking him up and down.

"A lot has happened."

His condition tugged at my heartstrings, and suddenly I wasn't so desperate to know what he wanted to tell me. "I think you need to go home and sleep. Maybe we should have this talk another day…"

He shook his head. "It's now or never."

It sounded serious. "What is it?" I held my breath.

"I thought you might have already found out. It's already been leaked to the media."

"I saw something on TV but didn't quite catch what it was about."

"You know the actor, Kim Jimoon? He has been having medical issues and had to drop out from his role in Love in Flames. Now I've been offered the part."

My muscles relaxed. It wasn't bad news after all. "Well,

that's great!—Except for Kim Jimoon and all. You were so upset that you missed out on that one."

"Yeah. But the thing is, it's so last-minute."

"Oh? How much time do you have?"

"Filming begins in two days."

I recoiled, startled. "Two days?!"

"And it's set on Jeju Island. They want me to go there tomorrow."

"Jeju Island?! Does that mean—"

He nodded. "They have a house rented for me for four months—I'll still be able to visit you from time to time, on my days off," he added, as if a consolation.

"I'm happy for you." My cracking voice betrayed my bitterness.

"Four months will go by before you know it," Jinseung assured me.

"Yes, I'm sure it will." *No, it won't. Four months is forever.*

Before embarking on this relationship, Jinseung and I had agreed that I wouldn't purposely interfere with his career, and I was more than happy to oblige. But now, faced with yet another prolonged period apart, it was difficult to keep my emotions reined in. As selfish as it was, I wished that he felt strongly enough about me that he would turn down the role. But who was I kidding? Acting was his first love, and I couldn't compete. Still, I didn't want to lose him, so I was required to put on a brave face and bear it.

"Are you okay?" Jinseung asked.

I forced a smile. "Of course. Why wouldn't I be? You've got the role you really wanted. We should be celebrating."

He squeezed my shoulder. "Thanks. I knew you'd understand. That's why our relationship works so well."

"What time will you leave tomorrow?"

"First thing. I'm off to Gimpo Airport at six o'clock."

"Then can I stay the night with you so I can say goodbye in the morning?"

"Sorry, but it would be more sensible if you didn't. I've got packing to do, and I need a good night's sleep tonight."

I pouted, unable to hide my disappointment. My bottom lip quivered. "Then this is the last time we'll see each other for a while…"

"Yeah." He stroked my cheek, a sympathetic look in his eyes. "Look at it this way, all this time apart will make our relationship stronger."

"I suppose so." *Or it could break us up…*

"I better head home. I need to prepare for tomorrow."

"But—"

He hugged me, muffling my protestation. "Be a good girl while I'm gone, okay?"

I sighed. "Don't worry. I won't get into any trouble."

"Good. I'll be in touch. Maybe not every day, but as often as I can."

"I'll be waiting to hear from you."

"I'm gonna miss you."

"Me too."

"Then…I'll head off now."

I bit back the urge to say, "I love you." He hadn't responded last time, and I couldn't face the same reaction this time.

Hands on my shoulders, Jinseung kissed me on the forehead one last time.

Jina coordinated his departure, checking that the coast was clear before permitting him to exit.

"Goodbye," Jinseung said, dropping his arms.

"Bye," I said weakly.

He turned, and without looking back, he left the building.

I watched the door swing behind him and close with a firm click.

I was unable to control the tears that suddenly leaked from my eyes. Jina caught me in her arms and let me cry into her shoulder.

"Don't tell Jinseung about this," I sobbed.

"I won't," Jina said, patting my back.

6

---

454 kilometres—the distance which now separated me and Jinseung. He had only been gone for a few hours, yet I could feel his absence in my very bones.

I didn't feel like doing anything that morning, not even getting out of bed. I pulled the covers up over my head to block out the sunlight and tried to fall back to sleep, but sleep didn't come. Begrudgingly, I pulled myself up and ate breakfast—cornflakes and milk.

After breakfast, I tried to do some prep work for my upcoming lessons, but my brain wasn't cooperating. I closed my laptop, deciding to go for a walk instead. Perhaps that would snap me out of this funk.

It was a clear day, the air brisk. I walked to a small neighbourhood near mine, where standalone houses replaced apartment buildings, some of them in a traditional Korean style with panelled walls and sloping roofs. I had always been fascinated by *hanoks* and had visited the *hanok* villages in Seoul many times. The houses in this neighbourhood weren't quite as impressive, but I still admired them. I wondered who lived in them. I imagined you'd have to be very rich to afford to live there. I watched the windows of the houses as I passed, hoping to catch a glimpse of their residents. I didn't see anyone in the houses, but a cat on top of a roof caught my attention—midnight black with vibrant yellow eyes. He looked like he was watching me.

"Here, kitty," I cooed, trying to get him to come down.

He didn't move. A sparrow landed on the roof next door and the cat's head snapped to attention. He leapt across to the other roof, but the bird flew away. I followed the cat for a while as he hopped from rooftop to rooftop until he eventually disappeared from view. At that point, I decided to head home.

When I reached my apartment building, I turned to the group of locked metal mailboxes beside the main entrance, deciding to check if I had any mail. I inserted the small key that I kept on a cute *Pororo* key chain.

My friend, Han Seri, and I had been writing each other letters, and I was expecting her latest piece of correspondence. We had been pen pals throughout high school to practise our language skills—I wrote in Korean, and she wrote in English. We had picked the habit back up in the last few months. It helped us to keep in touch, seeing as I wasn't going on social media often these days. After the "scandal" that occurred when the media released pictures of Jinseung and I together before we were even officially dating, I received a lot of hateful comments and DMs. The experience had put me off social media, and I rarely checked my accounts.

Sure enough, inside the metal mailbox was an envelope. I fished it out, recognising Seri's handwriting immediately. Envelope in hand, I went up to my apartment. I made a cup of tea before sitting down to read it, tearing open the envelope. The letter was written on thick, cream-coloured notepaper.

Dear Chloe,

Thanks for your letter. I'm so happy to hear that you're doing well. Seems like you have settled into teaching life quite well by now. I can't blame you for feeling uneasy at first. It's a big change from acting.

I have been watching Shin Jinseung's drama. I'm addicted! And he's soooo cute. I still can't believe that you're actually dating him. You lucky thing. In your letter you complained that you don't get to see him much due to filming. That must really suck. By the time you receive this I suppose filming will have already wrapped, so you'll get to see more of each other—for the time being, at least. Let me know how he's doing.

I have quite a bit of news to share this time. Guess what? I'm dating someone! He's an Australian guy, tall, good-looking. He works for an IT company. His name is Adrian. I've never felt this way about a guy before. It's only been a month and I'm already fantasising about marrying him! But there's a problem…

Remember how I told you last time that I was thinking about quitting my job and moving back to Korea? Well, now that I'm with Adrian, I'm not sure if I still want to. I can hardly ask someone I've only been dating for a month to go back to Korea with me, so we would have to have a long-distance relationship—or break up. I'm not too keen on that and I'm sure he wouldn't be either. That's why I'm having second thoughts about the whole idea.

I already told my parents that I wanted to come back to Korea, and they were so happy and excited. I'm not looking forward to telling them I've changed my mind. They'll be devastated. Then there's you, of course. We were thinking about moving in together if I came to live in Seoul. I still think that would be awesome, but it doesn't seem like that will happen now. I'm sorry.

Even if I don't leave Melbourne, I'll want to look for another job. Part of the reason I wanted to leave was that I'm not enjoying it. Don't know how much longer I'll be able to stick it out. Thank goodness I didn't already give my notice, though. Much like you, I need a job or I'll lose my visa.

Hope everything's okay with you. Give Jinseung a kiss for me! Ha! Just because I have a boyfriend now doesn't mean I'm not jealous.

Write back soon.

Your friend,

Seri Han

I folded the letter up and stuffed it back into its envelope. So, Seri had a boyfriend. I was happy for her, yet a little melancholy. Our plans to live together didn't look like they would pan out. *Never mind.* She hadn't had a boyfriend in a long time, so it made sense that she wanted to give their relationship a proper chance.

I sent a text message to Seri telling her I had received her letter. We always did so in case our letters ever got lost in the post.

My phone pinged a little while later, and I picked it up expecting to see Seri's reply. Instead, I saw a message from an anonymous sender. My breath caught in my throat.

Unknown: BREAK UP WITH SHIN JINSEUNG.

7

———

I was too overwhelmed by the mysterious text message to begin to try and make sense of it. The only thing I could think to do was to reply. Hand shaking, I composed a message.

Chloe: Who is this?

I watched anxiously as my message turned from "unread" to "read," then as the three little dots indicated the person was typing their reply. Even though I was expecting it, the pinging sound of a new message still gave me a fright.

Unknown: YOUR ENEMY

My blood turned cold. *My enemy?* Not knowing what else to say, I replied with a single question mark. Silence followed, and I didn't try texting them again.

Who could possibly send me such a message? No one knew about my relationship with Jinseung apart from a few close confidantes, and I was sure none of them would claim to be my enemy. Unless someone else had found out—a possibility I couldn't ignore. We had been very careful, but perhaps not careful enough…

I wondered whether I should tell Jinseung. He would surely be very busy preparing to shoot the drama, and I didn't want him to worry about me. Maybe this was all nothing—a disgruntled fan who still believed the old dating rumours and somehow got my number. *Yeah, that could be it.* Satisfied with my conclusion, I decided to ignore the message, block the number, and not tell Jinseung. I hoped the incident would be a one-off.

Only it wasn't a one-off. Similar messages started flowing in over the next few days. All of them a variation of "Break up with Shin Jinseung." Whenever I blocked the sender, they came through from a different number. I could no longer ignore them. I needed to confide in Jinseung and hear his opinion on the matter. Should I be concerned or not?

Predictably, I couldn't get through when I tried to call him. I left him a message instead.

> **Chloe:** Call me when you get the chance. I have something to tell you.

I waited for several hours, but he didn't reply. *Is he ignoring me?* I wondered, beginning to get frustrated. More "break up with Shin Jinseung" messages appeared in the meantime. I tried to call him once again, pacing the room while I listened to the dial tone. To my surprise, someone picked up, but the person who answered wasn't Jinseung. "Bong Changsoo here," the voice said.

"Changsoo-ssi, it's me, Chloe. Why do you have *Oppa's* phone?"

"I took it from him. He needs to be completely free of distractions today."

"Oh. I see." *So that's why he hasn't been replying…*I berated myself internally for believing that Jinseung was wilfully ignoring me.

"It seems like you're desperate to get hold of him. Is something wrong?"

"Yes. A situation has come up."

"I'm all ears."

I told him about the text messages and asked for his advice, praying he wouldn't be angry that the relationship might have somehow leaked out.

Changsoo paused. He breathed heavily down the line, apparently thinking the situation through. At last he spoke. "How likely do you think it is that this person could know you're dating?"

"I don't think it's very likely. We've done everything we can to keep it a secret."

"You haven't told them anything, have you? You haven't been replying?"

"I sent one message asking who they are, but that's it."

"In that case, I think the best course of action is to ignore the messages. Block the sender."

"I tried blocking them, but more messages come through from different numbers."

"They'll stop eventually if you don't engage with them. You've heard the expression 'don't feed the trolls,' right? This person sounds like a troll, trying to provoke a reaction from you."

"What if they really know about me and Jinseung? What if they leak it to the media if I don't respond to them?"

"We'll just have to take that risk."

It wasn't the reassurance I was hoping for, but I knew he

was right. "Okay." I sighed. "I'll do as you say and ignore them."

"Good. Don't delete the messages, though. Keep them as evidence. Unlikely as it is, you might need to show them to the police if the harassment escalates."

"Yes. Good advice."

"Thanks for letting me know about this."

"I'm just glad to get it off my chest. I wasn't sure what to do. Thank you."

"No problem. If anything like this happens again, let me know. It's best not to get Jinseung involved. He needs to focus right now and doesn't need this kind of stress."

I agreed with him. Jinseung was working hard and I didn't want to upset him. I'd deal with it myself, and with the help of Changsoo if necessary.

I left the phone call feeling a bit better about the whole situation, but not much clearer on the intention of the person behind the messages—*my enemy*.

Sticking to Changsoo's advice, I blocked the latest number that the messages were coming from but didn't delete them. *Keep it as evidence.* Where had I heard that before? *That's right.* Changsoo had advised Jinseung to keep the doll as evidence. The doll...the text messages. I wondered if there could be a connection between the two. What if the person in the motorcycle helmet who delivered the box to Jinseung's apartment was the very same person who was sending me these messages? Almost as soon as the idea entered my head, I dismissed it. *Don't be ridiculous.*

8

One evening at the *hagwon,* I noticed something on my desk that wasn't there before. The three novels I had recently lent Sophie had been stacked in a neat pile. *Has she finished them already?* On closer inspection, the stack was topped with a note written on rose-patterned stationery and a tiny pale blue box wrapped in a brown ribbon branded La Maison du Chocolat. My mouth dropped open a little. *Is this for me?* I unfolded the note. A message was written in beautiful handwriting with a blue-ink pen.

Dear Ms. Gibson,

Thank you for letting me borrow these books. I had a very nice time reading them. Slowly I am getting better at reading in English. Thank you for teaching me.

Yours sincerely,
   Kim Sungmi (Sophie)

Tears sprang to my eyes and I shielded my face, blinking them away before anyone could notice. I was so touched by Sophie's sweet gesture. It was the first time I had ever felt valued as a teacher. I lowered the note and met Sophie's eyes across the classroom. She swiftly averted her gaze, her cheeks pinkening.

I taught with much enthusiasm that day, and I was sad when class was over.

The students filtered out, leaving me alone to my thoughts. I had been avoiding checking my phone over the last couple of weeks, worried I'd see more anonymous text messages, but I couldn't stop looking altogether. What if someone was trying to contact me? I held my breath as I checked my messages, expecting to see a bunch of new ones. But nope. Not one. None from "my enemy." None from Yang Bora or Han Seri. None from Jinseung. I put my phone down feeling vaguely disappointed. Sure, the creepy text messages had stopped, but so had the texts from the people I cared about. The lack of contact from Jinseung hurt me the most. He had barely talked to me at all since he left. I knew he was busy, but still…

His words echoed in my head. "I'm a bad boyfriend." I had denied it at the time, but if he kept this up, perhaps I would start to agree with him.

I went to the staffroom, where I turned my attention to the latest batch of marking I needed to complete. Red pen in hand, I got to work. It took my mind off Jinseung, at least.

After an hour engaged in correcting and commenting on student work, I began to get drowsy. I stopped and gathered my papers up into my briefcase, calling it a night.

I felt a rush of cold air as I left the building. A lone student stood outside in the dark. It was Sophie, huddled in her jacket and rocking on her heels, glancing at her phone every few seconds. I approached her. "Everything all right?"

She lifted her head. "Oh, Ms. Gibson. I'm okay, but it doesn't seem like my mother will be able to pick me up."

"How will you get home?"

"Don't worry. I can take the bus."

"I'm just about to head to the bus stop myself. Which bus do you take?"

"76."

"Same as me! Do you want to walk together?"

"Yes, please!"

We left walking side by side along the footpath, bathed in the light from shop windows and glowing signs. The area bustled with groups of salarymen letting off steam after a long day's work.

"I want to thank you for the note and the gift," I said. "I wasn't expecting anything in return for lending you those books."

Sophie shrugged. "I just wanted to show you my appreciation. I've never had a teacher like you before."

"Really? You're the only student who seems to pay attention to me. I often wonder whether I'm any good at teaching at all."

"Don't mind the other students. They're just worn out from all the studying. There's so much pressure."

"Yes. You're right. It's very tough being a student in Korea. I studied here for one year on a high school exchange, but as a foreigner, I didn't face the same kind of pressure as the other students. How do you cope, Sophie?"

She thought for a moment before answering. "Ever since I was in primary school, I've been focused on my goal to study abroad, so I've never been concerned with the competition to get into Korean universities."

"Ah, I see. Though it can be challenging to get into over-seas universities as well."

"I know. That's why I think you can help me."

We reached the bus stop, but the number 76 bus was already pulling away from the curb, indicator flashing.

"Wait!" I yelled, flailing my arms, but it was too late. I had missed the bus many times recently. It was starting to become a habit. "The next one won't be for a while…"

"I will wait," Sophie said, unfazed.

I would have walked home, but I didn't want to leave Sophie waiting at the bus stop by herself at this time of night. Instead, another solution entered my head. "Sophie, do you like cake?"

Her eyes lit up. "I love it."

I took her to a nearby dessert café. Its interior was warm and inviting, softly lit, with framed poetry decorating exposed brick walls. An array of decadent cakes and pastries was displayed in a vast glass cabinet.

"What would you like?" I asked her.

"Hmmm…" She scanned the cabinet, her finger tracing her gaze across the glass. "Mont Blanc, please."

I ordered and paid for a slice of Mont Blanc cake for Sophie, and a slice of red velvet cake for myself

We crossed patterned rugs to a two-person table by the window, overlooking the hustle and bustle of a busy pedes-trian square.

"Now, what were we talking about before?" I asked. "Oh, that's right. Studying abroad. Do you have a particular university in mind?"

"Yes," Sophie replied. She looked down at the table, blushing. "It's my dream to go to Oxford."

Although it was an obvious choice, her answer still

surprised me. "Why Oxford?" I asked after taking a small bite of moist cake.

"My parents took me to visit England when I was little. I fell in love with Oxford, and it's been my dream to go there ever since. Think I just find the whole idea very romantic. The history, the architecture, the library, and the gardens…" She let out a little sigh of longing. "Have you been?"

"Yes. Several times. I even applied to study there, but I didn't get in. Ended up going to the University of Sussex instead."

"I know it'll be tough to get in. That's why I need to think about other universities as well, just in case."

"I could recommend some, depending on what you want to major in."

"I care more about where I study, rather than what I study. Certain programmes are easier to get into than others. That will influence my choice."

"I get what you mean. Picking something unpopular could make it more likely that you'll get into your preferred school."

"Exactly. What did you study?"

"Business."

"Oh?"

"A boring, practical option, which I'm not sure I'll ever make proper use of," I lamented. "If I could go back in time, I'd choose something else. Maybe Asian studies due to my interest in South Korea. Or possibly Korean language. Or maybe even acting…"

"Acting?"

"Didn't you know? I had a small part in a K-drama last year."

Sophie's jaw gaped. "Wow! That's so cool! What's it called?"

"Hidden History."

"I'll check it out."

Due to the small nibbles we took while conversing, we still hadn't finished our cake by the time we had to leave. A kind staff member boxed up our leftovers to take with us.

We walked back to the bus stop and joined the crowd of waiting passengers. The bus rolled up shortly. I found a free seat near the front, and Sophie sat down beside me. Just before the bus was about to leave, an elderly lady slowly climbed on board. Sophie readily gave up her seat to her. "Thank you, child," the *halmoni* said with a crinkled smile.

I gazed out the window throughout the short journey, watching the colourful storefronts and crowds of pedestrians go by in the night. When my stop neared, I pressed the red button. "Bye, Sophie. See you tomorrow," I said before hopping off.

While I made my way home, I thought about how Sophie reminded me of myself when I was her age—but a touch more romantic, intelligent, and sophisticated. I wondered whether she'd truly be able to get into Oxford. One thing was for sure, I was determined to help her succeed in her dream.

Shortly after arriving home, I rummaged through the fridge looking for something to cook for dinner and emerged with a pack of minced beef and some leftover chopped vegetables. I heated some oil in a frying pan then tossed everything in. As I prepared the stir fry, my phone started to ring. An unknown number, but I answered it anyway, pressing the phone to my ear with my shoulder. Due to the splattering, sizzling sound of oil, I couldn't hear properly. I removed the pan from the heat and listened more intently. What I heard disturbed me greatly. A computer-generated voice repeated the same message over and over again in a loop: "I'm warning you. Break up with Shin Jinseung or else."

9

I woke in a hot sweat during the night, a loud, piercing sound reverberating in my eardrums. Feeling dazed, I couldn't work out where the noise was coming from. Then I noticed my phone lit up on the bedside table. I rubbed my blurry eyes and focused on the screen. It was the same number calling me—the one which played the weird looping message: "I'm warning you. Break up with Shin Jinseung or else."

I groaned. *Not again.* I swiped to decline the call.

No sooner had my head touched the pillow than the ringing started again. I sprang back up and rejected the call. Fed up with the rude interruptions, I navigated through various menus and options to place a block on the number, then lay my head down again.

The rest of the night went uninterrupted, but I tossed and turned, unable to sleep. My mind raced. The doll, the text messages, the looping phone call…Were they connected? Was the same person behind all of these incidents? I was beginning to believe they were.

I had let Changsoo know as soon as I received the first phone call. His belief was that the person was trying to provoke me. He advised me not to do anything—yet. *Easier said than done.* I was starting to get scared. What else was this person capable of? A deep shudder trailed down my spine and I turned over, hugging the blankets around me more tightly.

A strong mug of coffee helped awaken my senses the next morning, sipped while I prepared a pot of Scottish-style porridge on the stove—a comfort food which I craved. How I wished I could confide in Jinseung about everything that had been going on. But Changsoo was right, he didn't need the stress right now. In the wake of these unusual events, I missed him even more. My whole body yearned for him. I texted him a simple message: "I miss you."

No reply came through all morning. It was like Changsoo said—he was too busy to pay me much attention.

Despite feeling less than stellar, I had to get on with my day. My cupboards were bare, and I needed to buy groceries. I grabbed my handbag and two reusable shopping bags and set out.

The sun beat down on the footpath filled with noisy groups of shoppers and tourists. Thanks to the anonymous messages and phone calls, my paranoia about being followed had returned. I stuck to the main streets, feeling safer among crowds.

I had just about reached the grocery store when a large digital screen on the side of a bus shelter caught my eye. I stopped. There was Jinseung, and alongside him was a devastatingly beautiful young woman. She had long wavy brown hair and a wispy fringe framing an angelic face with doe eyes and plump pink lips, a cute button nose, and a pointed chin. I realised she must be his costar in Love in Flames—Ahn Jieun.

They posed together, eyes locked on each other. Jinseung had a mischievous smirk on his face, and Jieun met him with a determined stare. The sexual tension between them was palpable. Below the image was the text: "Love in Flames—Coming soon to J2CB."

I felt a stab of jealousy through my heart. Unable to look at it anymore, I tore myself away.

———

I lost myself down a rabbit hole that afternoon.

Curious about Jinseung's hot costar, I typed her name into a search engine. A host of stunning photographs and video thumbnails popped up on the results page. The familiar stab of jealousy pierced my chest. *Damn. She's absolutely gorgeous. I'm seriously up against this? No man would be immune to her good looks...*

Scanning through the rest of the search results, I quickly learned that she was more famous as an idol rather than an actor. She was in a girl group called "Bad Grlz." I had heard of them before but didn't know anything about them. I clicked through to a profile of the group and found out that it consisted of five members, and Ahn Jieun was the leader. All of them were drop-dead gorgeous, not to mention talented. They wrote and produced all their own songs, as well as running a small clothing line and beauty brand.

After reading their profile, I found myself watching their music videos. Catchy pop songs with a slight hip-hop edge, featuring lots of sexy dance moves. Leading on from those videos, I watched interviews and dance practice clips. Next thing I knew I was on V Live watching the girls chat to their fans—a group called "Dollz."

Hours passed as I consumed Bad Grlz content in a trance,

envy seeping through every pore in my body. *Why do I have to torture myself like this?*

When I finally couldn't take any more, I shut my laptop and put it away in a drawer. I marched to the pantry and took out a jumbo bag of chocolate chip cookies which I proceeded to binge-eat. Between every few bites, I checked my phone, hoping that Jinseung would reply to me.

At last, my phone pinged.

Jinseung: I miss you too.

A wave of relief swept over me and I resolved to stop eating, but when I looked in the bag, I saw that it was empty. I had eaten all the cookies. A deep sense of shame replaced my relief as I brushed the crumbs off my sweater.

10

———

Dear Seri,

Sorry it has taken me so long to reply! I ran out of letter stationery and kept forgetting to buy more.

So you have a boyfriend now. Congratulations! I totally understand why you would want to stay in Melbourne to be with him. It sucks that we won't live together after all, but I'm still really happy for you.

By now I'm sure you know that Jinseung has left me to go film Love in Flames on Jeju Island. Once again, I find myself in a situation where I hardly see or hear from him. I know he's working hard, and I'm really proud of him, but it's still difficult. Then there's the fact that his costar, Ahn Jieun, is incredibly gorgeous. Have you heard of her? She's an idol in the group Bad Grlz. Everyone online is commenting on their chemistry. I'm not usually the jealous type, but this time I admit I'm feeling jealous.

There's another thing. I've been getting anonymous text messages and phone calls telling me to break up with Jinseung. It's pretty freaky. I'm not sure there's much I can do for now except ignore them. I haven't told Jinseung about them because it could distract him. There's nothing he could do anyway, so why bother him with it? I'm trying not to let the messages get to me, but I can't help feeling a bit paranoid. Sometimes I even feel like I'm being followed, but I have no solid proof of that.

There you have it. You have no reason to be jealous of me. In a way, I envy you for having a "normal" boyfriend. Things would be so much easier.

Hope everything is going well with Adrian and good luck job hunting.

-Chloe Gibson

———

I pushed the envelope through the post box slot and watched it disappear, wondering if its contents would still be relevant by the time it arrived in Han Seri's hands. Corresponding by letter was a bit like time travel, I mused. My life would move forward while the letter stayed the same. It landed inside the box without a noise, never to be seen by my eyes again.

With that taken care of, I walked down the subway station steps to board a train. I had arranged to meet Yang Bora at Cinema Lumiere.

A handful of moviegoers occupied the cinema lobby. Though there weren't too many people, the small space felt lively. The sound of chatter and the smell of popcorn filled my senses. I spotted Bora looking at the "coming soon" movie posters.

"Hey," I said, going to her side.

A smile spread across her round face. "Movie date time!" She linked her arm with mine.

We joined the short queue for tickets where Shin Jina manned the counter wearing a white blouse and bright pink lipstick.

"Hi, Chloe," Jina said when we reached the front. "Two complimentary tickets for The Strangers?"

"Yes, please!"

"Who's your friend?"

"Oh! This is Yang Bora. She works at KAM."

"Ahhh. The intern, right?"

Bora shook her head. "I'm Go Yoojin's manager now."

"Go Yoojin? Wow. That's cool."

"Yeah. She's great. A handful at times, though."

"I can imagine." Jina passed us the tickets. "Can you both stay a while after the movie? Let's chat."

"Sure," I said. "If it's okay with Bora."

"Yep," Bora said. "I don't need to be at work early tomorrow."

"Great," Jina said. "Enjoy the film!"

Tickets in hand, Bora and I entered the darkened movie theatre.

———

We emerged from the theatre two hours later and sat at a table while the other moviegoers slowly filtered out of the cinema. Once everyone had left, Jina joined us at the table with a bottle of white wine and three wine glasses. She filled them up.

Bora and I accepted a glass each, thanking her.

"So, Yang Bora, how long have you been working at KAM Entertainment?" Jina asked, sipping wine.

"Just about two years now," she said.

While Bora and Jina acquainted themselves, my phone

buzzed. I checked it, groaning internally at the sight of another "break up with Shin Jinseung" message. I slipped it back into my pocket, but every couple of minutes, it buzzed again. I pulled it out to turn it off.

"So, who's texting you?" Jina asked before I could press the power button. "My brother?"

I shook my head.

"Who is it then?"

"Actually…"

Bora and Jina stared at me, suspicion in their eyes. If I lied about the messages, they'd be able to tell. There was little use in hiding the truth from them anyway, so I showed them the messages.

Both of them squinted at the screen, shocked looks dawning on their faces.

"*Omo*!" Jina gasped.

"How long has this been going on?" Bora asked.

"A few weeks now," I admitted. "I've been getting phone calls too."

"You don't think…" Bora trailed off.

"What?"

"Is it the same person who delivered the doll to Jinseung?"

She was much sharper than me, making that connection almost instantly.

"The doll?" Jina's eyes widened in confusion.

"Some *sasaeng* fan delivered a mutilated Barbie doll to Jinseung's apartment," Bora explained.

"Yikes. That's disturbing."

"It might be the same person," I said. "I'm not sure."

"Does Jinseung know about the messages?" Bora asked.

I shook my head. "Bong Changsoo knows. He told me not to tell Jinseung."

Jina looked startled. "Eh! Why?"

"He'll be distracted from his work if he gets worried about me. Besides, it's not like there's anything he can do about it."

She pursed her lips. "Hmmm…I guess you're right. Though I'm sure Jinseung wouldn't agree with that."

"Please don't tell him."

"I won't."

"Same," Bora said. "I can see Changsoo's point. Jinseung's got enough to deal with as it is. I assume you've seen that recent article."

"What article?" I asked, concern in my voice.

"You don't know? The one about Ahn Jieun."

Ahn Jieun…My heart started to pound. What was this all about? "I haven't seen it."

"I'm sure it's nothing to be worried about. Just the media trying to stir things up, as per usual." She brought the article up on her phone. "Here, see for yourself."

I grabbed her phone and read the title. "Ahn Jieun and Shin Jinseung: Lovers Reunited." I gulped, my worst suspicion confirmed. I read on.

Ever since actors Ahn Jieun and Shin Jinseung started working together on upcoming drama, Love in Flames, fans have been ahuzz about the sizzling chemistry between the pair.

An exclusive source reveals that their chemistry might not just be good acting. It turns out that Ahn Jieun and Shin Jinseung share some history—they used to date!

Will their reunion reignite their passion? Our source on set thinks so. The pair have been spending a lot of time together, both on set and off.

Judge for yourself if their love is real when Love in Flames starts to air in June.

Several photographs of Jinseung and Jieun together behind the scenes accompanied the piece, as well as a photo that looked like they were having dinner together in a restaurant.

I set Bora's phone down on the table, unable to look anymore. The rational part of my brain agreed with Bora—it was just the media trying to stir things up and create publicity for Love in Flames, but the irrational part of my brain screamed louder, jealousy bubbling up inside me. I tried not to let it show.

"Like I said, it's nothing to be concerned about," Bora said, taking back her phone.

"Is it true that they used to date?" My voice wobbled.

"I don't know," Bora said with a shrug.

Both of our gazes turned to Shin Jina. If anyone knew, she would.

"It might be true," she admitted. "They used to spend a lot of time together. That was before either of them became famous. They were both trainees at the time. If they did date, I'm sure it was nothing serious. You shouldn't worry about it."

But I was worrying about it. Ahn Jieun was absolutely gorgeous and leagues ahead of me in talent and accomplishments. I gulped my wine down so fast I started to cough.

Bora rubbed my back soothingly. "Jinseung would never cheat on you."

"Yeah. He's not that kind of guy," Jina agreed.

"I know, but he's practically been ignoring me since he left for Jeju," I grumbled. "How does he have time to spend with Ahn Jieun off set when he doesn't even have time to contact me?"

"I'm sure the article's exaggerating. I know he's busy. He hasn't been responding to my messages either."

"You know what the media's like, Chloe," Bora said. "Just ignore it."

I did know what the media was like, but that did little to reassure me. When photographs of me and Jinseung hugging and holding hands came out last year, we weren't *officially* dating, but we weren't just friends either. *There's no smoke without fire.*

11

I took a deep breath before stepping on the scales in my bathroom. The number on the display shot upwards, then moved erratically up and down before settling on a final figure. I gulped down a lump in my throat. I was the heaviest I'd ever been. Thanks to the stress of the anonymous messages and the jealousy and worry about Ahn Jieun, I had been engaging in a lot of comfort eating lately. I stepped off the scales, making a promise with myself to cut back on the junk food. If Jinseung saw me like this, I'd be so ashamed. I needed to get back in shape before the next time we met.

I was about to leave the bathroom when I caught my reflection in the mirror and did a double-take. *Ugh. My skin.* I peered closer at the mirror. There was a massive lump on my forehead—a pimple under the skin that was threatening to burst forth at any moment. I supposed this was also a result of my unhealthy eating habits. *Don't touch it*, I told myself. *Do...not...touch...*I touched the spot, just lightly, but it was enough to turn it from skin-coloured to light pink. I lowered my hand. *See what you did?* Restraining myself from touching it again, I covered the spot with a light layer of foundation. It wasn't completely invisible, but no one would notice from a distance.

I got changed for work in my bedroom, pulling on a pair of smart grey trousers and a silky light pink blouse. Perhaps it was just my imagination, but the clothes did seem much tighter than usual. The waistband of the trousers cut into my stomach causing a muffin top, and the fabric between the buttons of my blouse gaped slightly. I realised I might need to buy more clothes, which would prove a challenge. By British standards I was small, but certainly not by Korean standards, so it would be difficult to find nice clothes that fit me properly. All the more reason to lose weight, I decided.

Ready for work, I grabbed my bag and headed to the door to leave when my phone started to ring. *Don't tell me it's another call from that weird stalker.* My hopes weren't high when I glanced at the screen, but to my surprise, the caller was Shin Jinseung. I couldn't believe it at first. When the shock wore off, I scrambled to answer the call before the ringing stopped. "Hello?"

"Hey, Chloe." His voice was raspy. He sounded worn out.

"*Oppa...*"

"How are you? I'm sorry I haven't been in contact. This has honestly been the most hectic drama I've ever worked on. You wouldn't believe how understaffed and overworked we are. I haven't had one day's break since we started. I'm not getting paid enough for this."

I didn't realise quite how busy he was until he divulged this. He gained my sympathy immediately. "That sounds tough."

"Are you okay? I have some time to chat with you a bit if you want. I've been missing you like crazy."

"Really?" Due to how busy he was, and how little he contacted me, I found it hard to believe he missed me.

"Of course."

"Thought you might be too busy to miss me."

"Even if I'm busy, I miss you."

I still wasn't convinced. The photographs of him looking cosy with Ahn Jieun surfaced in my mind. Before I could help myself, the question I had been desperately holding back surged forth. "What about Ahn Jieun?"

He paused. "Huh? What do you mean?" His tone of voice shifted from calm to irritated.

"It seems like you're close. Is it true that you used to date?" I tried to sound calm and reasonable, but it came out sounding more accusing than I intended.

He hesitated. "What have you heard?"

His reaction didn't comfort me at all. "I read it online. I wasn't sure if it was true or not."

He was silent, breath slow and steady.

"Say something," I urged, growing worried. "Tell me it's not true."

"That would be a lie."

His words hit me like a physical blow to the stomach, knocking the wind out of me. I had to sit down. "So, it's true," I said, voice cracking.

"Yes. We dated. It was a long time ago. I hadn't even debuted at that point—"

His protestation did little to soothe my flaring anger. "Is she the reason why you don't answer my messages?"

"What? Chloe, you've got the wrong idea."

"She's very pretty…"

Jinseung raised his voice. "Do you think I'd cheat on you? Is that what this is about?"

"I don't know," I bit back. "You don't love me. Maybe you love her?"

Fury laced his voice. "Ugh. I can't believe I'm hearing this. Perhaps I was wrong about you. I thought you could handle this relationship."

It was the first time I'd heard him this angry. I opened my mouth to try and take back the things I said, but I could only splutter unintelligibly.

"I've had enough of this," he said.

The call cut out.

———

After holding back my tears all evening, the dam finally burst. Before any students or colleagues could see me, I rushed to the bathroom and hid inside a stall, tears rolling uncontrollably down my cheeks. *Have I ruined everything? Is this the end? Jinseung must hate me now.*

Sitting on the toilet seat, I bent over my knees and buried my face in my hands. I wished I could retract the things I'd said. By revealing my insecurity and distrust to Jinseung, I had shown him that I wasn't fit to be his girlfriend. If he didn't have an excuse to leave me for Ahn Jieun before, he did now. A loud whimper escaped my mouth at the onset of a fresh round of tears.

The bathroom door creaked open, and I quickly covered my mouth with my hand to stifle the whimpering. I heard footsteps across the lino floor and a stall door open then close with a thunk. I bit my tongue, trying to be silent. If the girl heard me cry, she might ask me what was wrong, and I had no intention of revealing my vulnerability to a student.

I waited for the telltale signs of her leaving—the sound of the tap running, the rustle of a paper towel, and the clack of the door shutting behind her. Breathing a small sigh of relief, I emerged from the stall to wash my tear-streaked face. Standing before the mirror, I groaned at my reflection. The monster of a pimple on my forehead was angry and inflamed. I could even feel it throbbing. No amount of foundation or concealer would cover it up now. I gritted my teeth, bent down over the basin, and splashed my face with cold water, washing away my tears and soothing my burning cheeks.

In the midst of my second splash, the bathroom door swung open again. There was no hiding now. I lifted my head and saw Sophie walk in. Her eyes fell upon me at once, a wrinkle of concern appearing between her brows. "Ms. Gibson! Are you all right?"

"I'm fine, thank you," I croaked.

The line between her brows remained, a sign that she was unconvinced. "Are you sure? You looked unwell during class."

"Maybe I'm coming down with something."

"Well, I hope you feel better soon." Her gaze lingered on me and I felt totally exposed. She knew I had been crying, I was sure of it.

"Good job on your homework, by the way," I said, trying to change the subject.

"Oh, thank you." She looked away, blushing.

We stood in awkward silence for a moment before she remembered herself and disappeared inside a stall.

I splashed my face one more time then patted it dry with a paper towel. Reviewing my appearance in the mirror, I decided that would have to do. Perhaps the massive pimple would serve as a distraction to the fact I looked like I'd been crying. Then again, I wasn't sure if that was better or worse.

I managed to make it through the bus ride home without crying again, merely sniffling a few times as if I had a cold.

No one seemed to notice anything amiss, and if they did, they ignored me anyway.

At home, with no energy to cook a proper meal, I forgot all about my resolution to eat healthier and grabbed a packet of instant ramen from the cupboard. While the noodles boiled, I checked my phone, hoping to see a message from Jinseung. Hoping to see an apology. Surely he was feeling as guilty as I was. But nope. No new messages. I swallowed my pride. *Looks like I'll have to be the one to make the first move.*

I spent several minutes trying to draft a text message that conveyed the depth of my remorse. While I worked on it, I forgot about the noodles until I heard hissing sounds indicating the pot had boiled over. I rushed to attend to it, removing it from the heat immediately.

I prepared the noodles and ate them while I continued a cycle of writing then deleting text messages. Nothing sounded right. At last, I settled on something simple: "I'm very sorry." I held my breath as I pressed send.

I kept checking my phone throughout the night, aching to see him accept my apology and forgive me. But he didn't reply. Not that night, the next day, or the rest of the week. My sadness turned to anger, and with each day that passed without a response, the anger simmered away until it threatened to reach boiling point.

12

———

Of all people, I thought Yang Bora would understand my situation and offer her sympathy. Turned out to be a different story.

We sat on the couch in my apartment, cups of tea in hand. A K-drama played in the background, but we weren't really paying attention. Instead, I spilled my guts to her, telling her all about my fight with Jinseung and bemoaning his treatment of me.

She listened with a neutral expression on her face. Her reaction confused me since I expected her to be more fired up about this, the same as I was feeling. "So, what do you think?" I asked when I had finished my rant. "Is Jinseung totally out of line or what?"

Bora thought for a moment, her face still inscrutable. "I'm afraid I'm going to have to side with Shin Jinseung," she uttered at last.

I was taken aback by her statement. How could she side with him? "What do you mean? I apologised to him and he hasn't even acknowledged it!"

"He probably still needs time to process his feelings. I'm sure he'll come around eventually."

"It's been days!"

She spoke calmly. "Can I be frank with you?"

"Of course."

"Low self-esteem, jealousy, clinginess…those traits are unacceptable in a relationship between a celebrity and a non-celebrity. I don't blame Jinseung if he's still angry at you."

I tensed up in reaction to her harsh words. "I'm not usually that kind of person."

"But you have to admit that your outburst was a bad look."

"I couldn't control myself. All the stress of what's been happening piled up and I snapped. The lack of contact from him hasn't helped. Since the doll incident, I would have thought he'd be checking up on me, making sure I'm okay. And I'm not."

"You can hardly blame him for that. He doesn't even know what's been going on."

"If he had kept in touch, I probably would have told him."

"You know how busy he is with the drama."

I slumped forward, feeling defeated. "I don't know what to do."

Bora placed a comforting hand on my back. "I'm sure he'll forgive you. Just wait and see. My advice would be to stop worrying so much and trust him. Stop trying to contact him and get on with your own life."

"Easier said than done," I mumbled.

"Well, if you can't do that then I don't think you should be together."

Her words stung. "You really think so?"

She nodded slowly. "That's the way it is."

I started to cry. I couldn't help it. Bora wrapped her arm

around my shoulders to try and console me, but I pushed her forcefully away. She dropped her cup of tea and it spilled all over her. She sprang up, her expression dark.

"Oh no! I'm so sorry." I grabbed a fistful of tissues from the box on the coffee table and tried to dab at her shirt.

"I should go," Bora croaked.

"I didn't mean to—"

She flung on her jacket and walked out in a huff, door slamming behind her.

I wept into my hands. Fighting with Jinseung was bad enough, now I had turned Bora against me as well. Worst of all, deep down I knew she was right. If I couldn't handle Jinseung acting alongside a beautiful costar, if I couldn't handle jealous fans sending me threatening messages, how could I continue to date him? But the thought of ending our relationship hurt even more than those things combined.

Only one thing could numb my state of mind—junk food. I scoured the pantry for any sweet or salty snacks I could get my hands on, coming away with a packet of honey butter chips, a bag of macadamia nut cookies, and a bar of milk chocolate. Oh, and I couldn't forget the tub of salted caramel ice cream in the freezer.

Arms full with my haul, I relocated to the couch and spread the goodies on the coffee table. With a mindless reality TV show blaring in front of me, I proceeded to eat my way through all of the treats.

Only a few minutes after I had finished stuffing myself, my stomach groaned. A wave of nausea swept over me. I ran to the bathroom as fast as I could, flung open the toilet seat, and puked into the bowl. I purged over and over until there was nothing left in me.

Trembling on the bathroom floor, I realised I had reached a

new low. *I can't go on like this.* Something had to change—and the most obvious answer was me.

13

———

I was ready to apologise to Bora, but she wasn't ready to listen to me. Much like the situation with Jinseung, my calls and messages begging for forgiveness went unanswered. Determined to see her and apologise face to face, I resorted to catching her unaware. I went to KAM HQ one day, hoping she'd be there rather than out on a shoot.

Standing in the sleek, glitzy lobby, surrounded by screens playing video clips of the agency's star talent—including Shin Jinseung, Go Yoojin, and another young actor I recognised called Jung Jen. An overwhelming feeling of nostalgia took hold of me. It wasn't that long ago that I used to be signed to KAM as an actor, but now that short period of time felt like a distant dream.

As I stood lost in thought, many familiar faces passed me by. I felt self-conscious. *They're wondering what on earth I'm doing here…No. They probably don't even remember who I am…*

Shrugging off my embarrassment, I strolled up to the reception desk.

"Can I help you?" the receptionist asked, her tone clipped.

"I would like to see Yang Bora if she's available."

She narrowed her eyes. "Is she expecting you?"

"No."

"Then I'm afraid I can't help you."

"But—"

"Due to her busy schedule, Yang Bora does not meet anyone without prior arrangement."

I dropped my head in defeat. "I see. Thank you."

Now what should I do? Wait in the lobby and hope she comes out? I couldn't stay all day since I had work that afternoon. Besides, it would look suspicious if I hung around too long. What if I got mistaken for a fan trying to catch a glimpse of one of the agency's stars? I cringed at the thought. Heaving a sigh, I started towards the exit.

"Chloe?" came a voice over my shoulder.

I turned to see Seo Minjung—the talent scout who originally spotted me all those months ago and set my acting fate in motion. She looked beautiful as always, with her polished hair and makeup, and a Chanel handbag tucked beneath her arm.

"Minjung-ssi…" I spluttered, lost for words.

"Haven't seen you for a while. What brings you here?"

"I was hoping to see Yang Bora."

"Oh. Does she know you're here?"

I shook my head. "If she knew then she'd avoid me. We had a fight, you see. I'm here to apologise. Have you seen her today? Is she in the office?"

"Yes, I've seen her. I can go get her if you want. She might be busy, though."

"I'm not sure if she'll agree to see me."

"I'll tell her there's someone waiting for her, but I won't say it's you."

"All right, then. Thank you."

"Just wait right here. I'll message you what she says."

"Perfect."

With that, she whisked herself away to the elevators.

I paced the floor, phone glued to my hand. Eventually, it pinged with a new message.

Minjung: She'll come down in a minute. Good luck!

I hovered around the elevators, watching for any sign of Bora. At last, she emerged. Our eyes locked and she froze. "What are you doing here?" she asked. "Wait—did you send Seo Minjung up to get me?"

"Yes. Sorry to bother you. I just wanted to apologise again. Face to face."

She pursed her lips. "I can't discuss this right now. There's so much to do." She turned on her heel.

Before she could fully turn around, I dropped to my knees in front of her to beg her forgiveness. "Please!"

Her steely facade melted away, replaced by a sheepish smile. "All right, all right! Get up." She pulled me up off the floor, flustered by my embarrassing display.

"You're a true friend, you know. I needed someone to be brutally honest with me like you did."

"I'm glad you realised that."

"I really want to talk with you. Have you got time? Are you about to have a lunch break?"

"No. I'll be eating lunch at my desk. But I can meet you after work. There's a *pojangmacha* nearby. What time do you finish work?"

"Nine or so."

"Meet me at around half-past, then."

My post-work meeting with Yang Bora couldn't come soon enough. The minute the last student left my class, I disappeared as well, taking the train back to Gangnam.

I located the *pojangmacha* easy enough. Bora, draped in a trench coat, stood outside waiting for me.

"Hey!" I said, walking up to her. "Hope you haven't been waiting long."

"Nope. Just got here."

We entered the bright orange tent filled with the fumes of salt and oil. It bustled with workers drinking alcohol and eating crispy, spicy, fried foods.

"What would you like?" I asked.

"*Sundae*," Bora replied.

"You eat that stuff?" I shuddered at the mere mention of the blood sausage dish.

"Of course."

"It makes me gag."

"You don't have to eat it."

"I'll get *tteokbokki* then. Anything to drink?"

"A beer, please."

I ordered the food and drinks, then we sat at one of the plastic tables. We were served two cold cans of Cass beer. I opened the cap on mine, and it made a "tsst" sound.

"So, what did you want to talk about?" Bora asked.

"Let's talk about you first. I've been so wrapped up in my own little world. I haven't been listening to your problems. How's everything with Go Yoojin?"

"She's started table reads for her next drama. Apart from that we're not too busy."

"Still giving you a hard time?"

"Always." She chuckled. "But I feel like she's grown to trust me now. We have a good relationship."

"I'm glad to hear it. Not missing working with Shin Jinseung?"

"Surprisingly, no."

Our food came—a bowl of rice cakes in spicy red broth, and the gross blood sausages I despised.

We snapped apart our chopsticks and began to eat.

"It's good," Bora said, mouth half-full. "Want to try some?"

I screwed up my nose. "No, thanks." I picked at my food, playing with it more than eating it. "I actually shouldn't be eating this. My diet has been terrible recently. I've put on so much weight and my skin is constantly breaking out."

"Not to be rude, but I've noticed you haven't been looking your usual self."

"I haven't been taking care of myself properly."

"All that stress, huh?"

"Yeah. I could really use your advice. I'm ready to listen to your opinions properly this time."

"You want me to be brutally honest?"

"Yes. Please go ahead."

"Promise you won't get angry at me?"

"I promise."

She came out with it at once. "I think you should consider breaking up with Jinseung."

My heart sank. It was not what I had wanted to hear, but I held back my gut reaction of defensiveness. "Why do you think so?"

"Think about it. Your relationship with him is the cause of all your problems. Breaking up with him would be the simplest solution."

"But not the only solution?"

"No, but the other way is more difficult. You'll have to overcome all your issues. Are you strong enough to do that?"

"I always believed I was a strong and resilient type of person, but now I'm not so sure…"

"Regardless of what you choose to do, I think you should come clean to Jinseung about the messages you've been getting."

"But Bong Changsoo—"

"Pfft. Forget about him. He doesn't have your best interests at heart. He only cares about preserving Jinseung's career for the sake of his job. Ignore him and come clean."

"That's not what you said before."

"The situation has changed. Jinseung needs to understand the stress you've been under and why you snapped at him."

"Then he might take pity on me…"

"Well, that's one way of putting it."

"…Or he might break up with me."

"He might break up with you either way, and this is the better option."

"Ugh. You're right. I guess I'll have to take the risk."

Bora's eyes fell upon the largely uneaten dish in front of me. "You gonna eat that?"

"Nah. You can have it." I pushed it towards her. My appetite had disappeared. If I had any chance of keeping my boyfriend, I'd need to quit my binge-eating habit.

"Man, I'm stuffed," Bora said, after managing to polish off a lot of what I didn't eat.

"You taking the subway home?" I asked.

"Yeah."

"Then let's go to the station together."

We stepped out of the warm tent and into the brisk night, navigating the streets to the nearest subway entrance. Our paths diverged inside the station, where escalators to the left and right led to separate train lines.

"I'm going left here," Bora said.

"Well, thanks for the chat. It's given me a lot to think about."

She beamed. "No problem. Any time."

"I don't know what I'd do without your friendship."

"Let's never fight again."

"Agreed."

We exchanged smiles, expressing contentment with our reconciliation, then headed our separate ways. I might not have been any closer to making up with Shin Jinseung, but at least I had Yang Bora by my side.

14

A chorus of groans reverberated through the classroom. I had expected such a reaction. No one likes a surprise test. "Don't worry," I said, trying to be reassuring. "There should be nothing unfamiliar on the test. Just give it your best shot. You have until the end of class to finish."

I walked around the room passing out the test papers. Some students accepted theirs with glum expressions, others with determination—including Sophie. After handing out the last paper, I returned to the front of the room. Everyone stared at me expectantly, pens at the ready, waiting for me to tell them they could start.

"You may begin," I announced.

A flurry of rustling paper and scratching pens took over the class. I sat down behind my desk and relaxed, my shoulders drooping. One good thing about tests was that I didn't have to do any actual teaching. I kept one eye watching the students at all times, making sure no one was cheating, but my mind wandered. I found myself absentmindedly reaching for my phone. One new message. Could it be from Jinseung? I swiped the screen, then deflated a little upon seeing Han Seri's name.

Seri: I got your letter. Hope everything is OK. My
    reply is already in the post.

I typed a response.

Chloe: I'm okay. I'll tell you everything in my next
    letter. Can't wait to read yours.

I returned my attention to the students. Their heads were down, faces etched with concentration. Sophie looked the most confident out of everyone, her tongue poking out slightly as her pen raced across the page. She was the first to lower her pen. After a couple of minutes reviewing her answers, she raised her hand.

"Are you finished?" I asked.

"Yes. What should I do now?"

"You can study quietly until the end of class."

I collected her paper. From a brief glance while carrying it to my desk, I could tell that she had done well. *I wonder if this class is too easy for her.* She was clearly leaps and bounds ahead of her peers.

A full fifteen minutes passed before the next person finished their test. Only a handful of other students managed to finish before I called "time's up."

I collected the rest of the papers then dismissed the class. As the room emptied, I regarded the intimidating stack of test papers on my desk. *This will take some time to mark.* I remembered the chicken and fresh vegetables I bought earlier that day, intending to prepare a healthy meal for dinner. If I stayed late marking, there was no chance I'd be bothered to cook when I got home. *The marking can wait*, I decided. If I made a big dinner tonight, I could bring the leftovers to eat tomorrow while I did the marking. Satisfied with this plan, I headed home.

Arriving at my apartment building, I checked my mailbox as usual. Seri's letter probably wouldn't arrive for another week or so, but I was expecting a credit card bill.

I reached my hand inside the mailbox—empty, apart from a folded piece of notepaper. *Hmmm, what's this?* I retrieved the piece of paper and carefully unfolded it. As soon as I read the note it slipped from my grasp as I reeled in shock.

I'M WARNING YOU AGAIN. BREAK UP WITH SHIN JINSEUNG.

A startling realisation dawned on me. *The stalker knows where I live.*

I stood frozen, head spinning. A gust of wind almost sent the note flying into the air, but I pinned it down with my foot just in time. I bent down to pick it up and tucked it away in my pocket—I needed to keep it as evidence.

Still in a state of shock, I wearily made my way up to my apartment. Once inside, I carefully looked around for signs of a break in. Since this person knew where I lived, it was entirely conceivable that they might have tried to gain entrance. They could even be hiding inside at this very moment...

So far, nothing looked out of place, but then a noise from the bathroom made me jolt to attention. I armed myself with a knife from the kitchen, then slowly approached the bath-room door. Hand shaking, I tightened my grip around the doorknob and twisted. I held my breath as I pushed the door open in a swift motion, expecting to catch a startled intruder.

But the room was empty. I was alone. I let out my tension in a long relieved sigh.

Before doing anything else, I set about changing my door code—the simplest safety measure I could take. I input my old combination into the keypad, then proceeded to set a new four-digit code. The digital lock played a short confirmation tune. *There.* Safe and secure.

———

If anything was going to reveal the identity of the culprit, it was the security footage from the camera at the building's entrance. I called the building manager the next morning, whose number I had saved on my phone in case of emergency.

"*Yeoboseyo?*" a pleasant-sounding woman answered.

"Hello. This is Chloe Gibson. I'm a resident of the Saim-dang building, apartment number 4C."

"What can I help you with?"

"I received a threatening note in my mailbox today. I wondered if you could review the security footage for me and see who placed it."

The woman hesitated. "Usually we only accept this kind of request from the police."

My resolve deflated. *Of course. They wouldn't just share the footage with anyone.* "I understand, but I don't know if this is serious enough to involve the police."

"Could I see the threatening note you speak of? You could send me a photo of it."

I considered whether or not to show her the note, after all, it did reveal my secret relationship. I had no idea whether I could trust the woman I spoke with. "It's...of a personal nature. I would rather not share it if possible."

"Then I'm not sure if there's much I can do. Sorry."

I didn't have time to change my mind. The woman promptly hung up.

I collapsed on my bed, groaning in frustration. *What should I do now? Contact the police?* I had evidence of harassment, but would it be enough? After all, no physical harm had befallen me…*yet*. There was also the risk of revealing my relationship in the process. *No.* The police should be a last resort, I decided. For now, I had to remain vigilant.

I spent the rest of the morning re-organising and backing up my file of evidence—screenshots of the text messages and call log, a recording of one of the phone calls, and a photograph of the note.

Maybe I should look into security systems as well. I checked out a website selling cameras, locks, and alarms. *This shit's expensive. What if I'm overreacting…*

My phone started to ring. *The building manager?! Did she have a change of heart?*

"Are you the person who called earlier about the security footage?" the woman asked.

"Yes."

"I had some time, so I decided to take a quick look."

My heart thudded in my chest. "Oh? Did you see anything?"

"There *was* a suspicious individual."

"Who was it? What did they look like?"

"It's clear that they don't want to be identified. They were wearing all black, and a motorcycle helmet over their head."

The significance of this development was not lost on me. "A m-motorcycle helmet?"

"That's correct. Is that useful information?"

"Yes. It is. Thank you."

'I'm glad I was able to help you. Sorry I can't provide any more details."

"That's all right. Thank you very much for letting me know."

A black outfit and a motorcycle helmet. That was enough to confirm my suspicions. My stalker was the same person who delivered the mutilated doll to Jinseung's house. A disturbed and possibly dangerous individual.

15

The tower of test papers leaned precariously in front of me, threatening to topple and cascade around the room. I deftly restrained the stack and rearranged it into three smaller piles.

Working kept my mind off the stalker, and I felt safe within the confines of the *hagwon*. I needed to get this marking done, anyway.

My last class for the day was over. I sat at a messy, overflowing desk in the staffroom, surrounded by utilitarian office furniture, shelves bursting with books and files, and equipment cords like snakes lying hazardously over the floor. I was alone, my only light source a desk lamp, plus the streetlight coming in through the gaps in the blinds.

I reached for Sophie's paper and opened it. Her handwriting was beautiful as usual. I read her answer to the first question and awarded her a red tick.

With each tick, I felt a growing sense of disappointment. Call it selfish, but I hoped she would get at least a few questions wrong. My hopes diminished as I neared the end of the paper. On the last page of the booklet, I wrote 100% and circled it. Time to face up to the reality of the situation— Sophie couldn't stay in my class any longer. She was finding it too easy and needed to be moved up to the advanced level. That meant I would no longer be her teacher. I let out a sigh, thinking how much I'd miss her. *It's for the best,* I told myself. Sophie needed to excel to get into Oxford, and that meant pushing her capabilities.

Over time, the piles in front of me dwindled, and at last, I left the building. I made my way to the bus stop, never straying from the main streets and always keeping a wary eye tuned in on my surroundings. I no longer considered it paranoia. There really was someone out there targeting me, possibly planning to harm me. I had to tread carefully.

I was near the bus stop when something caught my eye, sending a wave of fear surging through my veins. A person who fitted the exact description of the culprit. They were riding a scooter, dressed in black, and with a black motorcycle helmet over their head. *Could it be?*

Before I could react, the scooter driver zoomed off and turned down a side street. My legs unfroze, and with a sudden spike of adrenaline shooting through my body, I ran after them. Now was my chance to possibly catch and identify my harasser.

The side street was long, dark, and narrow. I could see the scooter driver in the distance, tail light shining.

"Wait! Stop!" I cried. I ran as fast as I could, but the gap between us widened. Nearly out of breath, I was about to give up the chase when a traffic light at the end of the road turned red and the scooterist stopped. *Now's my chance.* I ran as fast as my legs would take me. *Almost there…*

My foot landed funny on the pavement. My leg gave out and I fell down with a smack. I lay helpless, head dizzy and my body throbbing with pain. When I finally gathered the strength to lift my head, I saw the helmeted individual walk towards me. Closer…closer…

"No!" I whimpered, shielding myself with my hands.

They reached out their hand to me. "Are you okay?" He lifted his visor, revealing a baby-faced young man—or boy—with big, wide eyes full of sincere concern.

The tension drained out of me as I let him help me up. "Yes, I'm okay." I brushed myself off.

"Were you following me?" he asked in heavily accented English.

"Yes. I thought you were someone…I must have been mistaken." It seemed unlikely that this boy could be my harasser.

"Be more careful, okay?"

I nodded and limped away, head hung in embarrassment. Emerging back onto the main road, I looked around and realised there were many people on scooters and motorcycles in the surrounding area—and several wearing black outfits and the same, generic helmet. I cursed myself for being so stupid. Of course I wouldn't be able to pick the culprit on that information alone. It wasn't nearly enough to go off.

I managed to get to the bus stop on time—barely. The driver had just closed the bus door, but I rapped on it, and it jerked back open. I hopped on board, panting, and dropped into the closest available seat.

My face stung. I gingerly touched my cheek. The skin felt rough and sore. I pulled a pink compact mirror out of my bag and examined my reflection. Sure enough, my face was grazed and tender along the left side, matching the state of my palms. I resolved to put some ointment on it as soon as I got home.

I got off the bus at my stop and walked briskly to my

apartment building. When I reached my door, I input the code on the digital lock. An error sound played. Thinking I had mistyped, I re-entered the code. It didn't work. Eventually, I remembered that I changed the combination the previous night. I closed my eyes and searched my brain, willing for the new code to surface in my memory. My mind was completely blank. It was no use. I was locked out.

16

———

There was a trick to opening locked doors that I had learned from movies. I pulled out my wallet and selected a random card. Not entirely sure what I was doing, I inserted the card into the narrow crack between the door and the frame and tried to run it through the junction where the lock bolted across. As soon as the card met resistance, I lost my grip. It slipped out of my hand and disappeared into the crack. *Damnit. Why did I use my main credit card?!* I didn't dare attempt the "trick" again, lest I lose another important card.

On to the next tactic. I tried a few different codes which I had used for other things in the past. No luck, and after several incorrect attempts, the digital lock wouldn't let me try again. "Arrggggh," I groaned.

Pacing the corridor, I racked my brain for what to do. I could call the building manager again, but I'd get charged a hefty lockout fee plus an after-hours surcharge. Besides, I was sure that given time, I would remember the combination.

I made up my mind to stay the night somewhere else, and

if I still couldn't recall the code by morning, I'd call the building manager and stump up the fee.

The most obvious place to crash was Jinseung's apartment, but could I risk going there when there was a crazy stalker bent on breaking us up on the loose? Not to mention they knew where it was and had managed to get up to it before. No, it would be more prudent to stay at a friend's house.

I scanned my eyes down the list of contacts on my phone, wondering who to call. My first choice was Bora, but she lived quite far away and with parents I had never met which made things awkward. I kept scrolling until another name jumped out at me—Shin Jina. I called her.

"Hello?" Jina said.

"*Unnie*, it's me, Chloe."

"Oh, Chloe! How are you?"

"Actually, I'm in a bit of a predicament."

"Is that so?"

I explained my situation to her, and she was more than willing to help.

"I'm at work right now," she said. "But if you meet me at the cinema, I'll take you to my place when I'm finished. Does that work for you?"

"Yes, it does. Thanks so much!"

"All right, see you soon."

"See you."

Continuing to exercise caution with my movements, I reached Cinema Lumiere by subway.

Jina was alone in the foyer when I arrived. She sat behind the counter, flipping through a glossy magazine, a bored expression on her face.

"Hey," I said, approaching her.

She looked up. "Hey!" Her dark eyes fell upon my cheek and she frowned. "What happened to your face?"

"Oh, this? I fell over."

"Ouch."

"Yeah."

"Falling over, then getting locked out of your apartment. Things aren't going well for you today, are they? How did you manage to lock yourself out, anyway?"

"I changed my door code yesterday and forgot what I changed it to. Stupid, I know."

"Why did you change it?"

"It's a long story."

"I'm intrigued. Tell me when we get back to my place, okay?"

"Okay." She was letting me stay the night at her house, the least I could do was give her the truth of the situation.

"The last screening is in session," Jina explained. "Once that's over, I just need to do a quick clean-up, then we'll go."

"Okay, no problem."

"Coffee?"

"Yes, please."

Jina prepared us a hot cup of coffee each, then she joined me at a table. By the time we had finished our drinks, the movie had finished. The moviegoers slowly filtered out while the credits rolled. I helped Jina tidy up. Cleaners would be in later to do a more thorough job.

At last, Jina turned off all the lights, set a security alarm, and locked the door. We walked to the subway station.

"I live in Hongdae," Jina explained. "It won't take long to get there."

I was very familiar with the young and trendy area of Seoul. At this late hour, the streets were still jam-packed with young people heading to bars and clubs. The lively atmosphere re-energised me.

Jina's apartment building was located near Hongik University. The low-rise building was a bit decrepit looking, but the interior had a lovely traditional Korean style with wooden floors, panelled walls, and sliding doors. The charming little apartment was cramped and a little messy, with piles of fashion magazines littering the floors and tons of clothes and papers strewn about

"Sorry, it's messy," Jina said, hastily removing the dirty dishes off the coffee table and dumping them in the already overflowing kitchen sink.

"That's all right. It's a cute apartment."

"Thanks. My flatmate lives here too. Her name's Scarlett. She's a model at the same agency as me." She knocked on Scarlett's bedroom door, but there was no answer. "Looks like it's just the two of us. Probably staying at her boyfriend's place. Make yourself comfortable."

I sat down on the living room couch. Jina disappeared for a second, then reemerged holding a tube of ointment. She bent down in front of me. "This will help your face heal." She squirted a little ointment into the palm of her hand, then gently applied it to my face. "There. That should do the trick."

"Thank you."

She put the tube away then entered the kitchen. "Would you like a beer?" She pre-emptively took two cans out of the fridge.

"Oh, yes, please. If you're having one."

She joined me on the couch and handed me a cold beer.

"So, I'm curious." She opened the tab on her can. "Why did you change your lock?"

I stroked the side of my neck, carefully thinking through how I would phrase my plight, but when I opened my mouth the words came tumbling out. "You know that person I told you about who's been harassing me with the phone calls and messages? I have a feeling they've been spying on me as well. Today they left a note in my letterbox, which means they know exactly where I live. I changed my door code as a precautionary measure."

Jina raised a hand to her lips and chewed her nails. "That's really freaky. They're like a stalker or something. I think you should tell my brother, if you haven't yet. He's involved in this. It's probably one of his fans doing it. He would want to know."

"I'm planning to tell him, but there's a problem. We recently had a fight. He hasn't been answering any calls or messages, and I don't want to pester him too much right now. I'm scared it's annoying him."

"A fight, huh? Was it about Ahn Jieun, by any chance?"

"Ugh. You guessed it."

"I figured you were probably jealous. Not to mention the stress of the stalker mixed in. It's no wonder you fought. But *Dongsaeng* doesn't know the whole story. If you told him about the stalker, I'm sure he'd be more understanding."

"That's what Yang Bora said too."

"He's not answering your calls, but maybe he'll respond to me. I can try my best to get through to him."

"You mean, you'll tell him what happened to me?"

"Yeah. If that's okay with you."

I chewed my lip, unsure. "I don't know…wouldn't it be better for him to hear it from me?"

"I'll just tell him the basic details and prompt him to call you. Then you can explain everything."

I still wasn't quite sure how involving Jinseung would help the situation, but for some reason it felt like the best way forward, and I knew Jina would handle the conversation with tact. I made up my mind. "Okay. Agreed."

Jina brightened. "Good. I'll try to contact him tomorrow. For now, you better get some rest. You look super tired."

"I feel super tired."

"You can sleep in my room."

"Are you sure?"

"Yup. I'll sleep in Scarlett's room. She won't mind." She led the way to her room and slid open the door.

Jina's bedroom was girly to the extreme. Her canopied bed overflowed with cushions and stuffed toys, and a string of fairy lights decorated the headboard. Opposite the foot of the bed was a dressing table covered with cosmetics and perfume bottles. A large mood board hung on the wall, made up of cuttings from magazines featuring beautiful women and inspirational quotes. The room smelled like hairspray, flowers, and scented candles.

Jina quickly scooped away a pile of clothes off the bed and threw them inside her wardrobe. "You have nothing to wear to bed, do you?" She ducked down and opened a drawer, rummaged a bit, then emerged with a pair of silky pink pyjamas. "Here you go. They're clean." She gave them a sniff just to double-check, then passed them to me.

"Thanks."

"Have a good sleep. See you in the morning."

"Night night."

She closed the door. I changed into the pyjamas, flicked off the light, and climbed into the bed, careful not to disturb her collection of plush toys.

Like most epiphanies, it hit me in the middle of the night as I was waking from a dream: the door code. I repeated it in my mind, willing myself not to forget it until I could write it down. I grabbed my diary, turned to a blank page, and quickly recorded it. I knew that it wasn't a good idea to write down your passwords or secret codes, but it's all I could think to do in the moment while sleepiness threatened to let the number slip from my mind again.

17

———

I held my breath as I input the door code, praying that my memory hadn't betrayed me. After I punched the last digit, a lengthy delay ensued until finally the door unlocked with a click. *Phew.* Home sweet home. My credit card was lying upside down on the floor. I bent down to recover it and slipped it safely back into my wallet.

I tried to keep busy that morning to stop myself from constantly checking my phone, wondering when or if Jinseung would contact me. The few times I did allow myself to take a peek, there were no new messages.

I still hadn't heard from him by the time I left for work. During my lessons, I kept my phone on my desk and occasionally glanced down to check it inconspicuously. A call came through mid-lesson, Jinseung's name on the screen. For obvious reasons, I couldn't answer. My break couldn't come soon enough.

At the end of the class, I looked for a private spot on the premises to call Jinseung back. After a quick look around the building, I decided that the balcony off the staff kitchen would suffice. I nipped out and closed the sliding glass door behind me. The balcony was very exposed, and the wind whipped at me. I pulled my hair back into a ponytail to keep it from blowing in my eyes. Without further hesitation, I made the call and pressed the phone hard to my ear so that I could hear through the street noise below.

Jinseung answered immediately. "Chloe..." His voice sounded husky with exhaustion.

I opened my mouth to respond but was unable to summon any words.

"Are you there?" he asked.

"...Yes."

"I don't know what to say except I'm sorry. *Noona* told me what you've been dealing with since I've been gone. I'm so sorry."

His sincerity quickly melted my icy facade. "I'm sorry too."

"What for?"

"Ahn Jieun—"

"Oh. Never mind that. It's understandable. You would have been so anxious and insecure with those messages hounding you. All the while I had no idea what was going on. I should have been more attentive—"

"It's not your fault," I cut in. "You're not psychic. How could you possibly know?"

"I need to come clean about something."

"What is it?"

"That day that I removed the doll...I found something else in the box. Something we didn't see before."

"Huh?"

"A note. It said 'Break up with Chloe Gibson.'"

I paused for a second, letting this new piece of vital information sink in. "What the hell? Why didn't you tell me?"

"I honestly thought it was just some jealous fan being a pain. I didn't want to concern you because I thought you'd overreact."

"It's not overreacting if it's a legit threat! This person could be really dangerous! You should have told me."

"And you should have told me about this too! Why didn't you?"

"I wanted to, but it's been hard to get hold of you. Plus, Changsoo told me not to."

"Changsoo did? Why would he?"

"He didn't want to cause you any stress."

"That's not his decision to make! Agggh I could murder him!" Rage coursed through his strained voice.

"I understood his point of view, though. What good does it do now that you know? You'll just worry and fret."

"I can help you."

"How?"

"I'll do something."

"What?"

"I don't know right now, but there must be something I can do. Perhaps a serious message to my fans. Perhaps…" He trailed off, then after a thoughtful pause he continued. "If you wanted to end things right now, I'd understand."

My throat turned dry. This was the line of thinking I was afraid he'd take. "No," I said resolutely. "I don't want to break up. No matter what happens."

"No matter what happens?" he repeated, voice tinged with uncertainty. "Okay…If you're sure."

"I'm absolutely sure."

He sighed deeply. "Chloe…I wish I could be with you and protect you, but I can't. I'm simply too deep into this project to quit now. I'd be letting everyone down—"

"I'm not asking you to do that."

"I know, but I've been asking myself if it's the right thing to do. At the moment it doesn't seem like you've been seriously threatened, but who knows what will happen. Be careful, okay? I've asked *Noona* to check up on you regularly and make sure you're all right. Also, I'd like you to stay at my apartment. The security is much better—"

"The security has already failed us once. The stalker knows where you live and knows how to get up to your apartment. It might make them angry if I stay there. I don't think I should risk it."

"If you're sure—"

I glanced at my watch. There was no more time to talk. "Jinseung-ah, I've got to go. My next class is starting in a minute."

"Promise me you'll be careful, and if anything else happens, you'll let me know?"

"I promise."

I ended the call and tucked the phone away in my bag. Was letting him know the right thing to do? I still wasn't sure, but at least we were both on the same page now.

The rest of the day's classes passed uneventfully until I saw Sophie arrive, and I remembered that I'd have to break the news to her—she would move to a different class from next week. I felt sad to lose her. We had formed a close connection somehow, and I couldn't imagine reverting back to pre-Sophie days at work.

At the end of class, the students began to leave in a flurry. I caught Sophie as she stood up and hauled her bag over her shoulder. "Sophie, can I have a word with you?"

"Of course." She put her bag back down.

I waited until we were alone, then took a seat near her. "You got 100% on the test. Well done."

She shrugged awkwardly but couldn't conceal her smile. "It wasn't difficult."

"This class must be too easy for you…"

She shook her head. "I'm still learning."

"I'm sure that's true, but it's clear to me that you would be better off in the advanced level. From next week, you'll move up a class."

"But…"

"You need to be in a more challenging environment. If you really want to pursue Oxford—"

"I'm leaving the *hagwon*," she interjected.

I paused, wondering if I had heard her correctly. "What?"

"My parents want me to have private tutoring instead."

"…I see." I rubbed my neck as I slowly absorbed this new piece of information.

"Will you do it?"

"What do you mean?"

"I want you to tutor me."

"That's—"

"My parents will pay you well."

Foreign English teachers weren't permitted to undertake private tutoring in Korea, but that didn't stop many from doing it since it was such a lucrative side gig.

"Think about it at least," Sophie urged.

I didn't need to think. I had already made up my mind. "I'll do it."

18

———

J inseung took action against my harasser using the most powerful weapon he had at his disposal—his platform. He posted a sad-faced selfie accompanied by a short message composed like a letter.

My dear fans,

How are you all? I hope you are eating well, staying fit, and getting plenty of sleep.

Unfortunately, I have some sad news. It has recently come to my attention that a so-called fan has been harassing someone close to me.

It makes me feel very upset that someone would do this—especially someone who is my fan.

My message to you is this: If you truly love me then you would never cause harm to my friends or family in any way—physically or mentally.

So I ask all of my true fans to leave my friends and family in peace, and to step in and stop anyone who behaves in such a horrible way.

It would make me so happy if you could support me with this.

Thank you for understanding.

Yours always,
Shin Jinseung

A long list of comments followed the post. I read the first few.

"That's awful. A true fan would never do this!"

"As fans we have to protect Shin Jinseung!"

"Nooooo. Poor Jinseungie."

"Whoever does this is not a real fan."

"Sasaeng fans are evil."

"Who dares to hurt Shin Jinseung?"

The post quickly became viral, being shared across K-drama groups and forums worldwide. If the person who was harassing me really was a *sasaeng* fan, then they definitely wouldn't miss it. Would it make them second-guess their behaviour? I could only hope so.

Several days passed with no new anonymous messages, and gradually I began to relax and let my guard down.

On a rainy Sunday afternoon, I walked to Booksea—the bookstore where I had agreed to meet Sophie for our first tutoring session. The huge, multi-floored bookshop housed soaring shelves full of titles in a vast number of genres and formats. Chandelier lighting suffused the store with a soft, warm glow, and the air smelled of coffee and fresh paper. An adjoining café furnished with mismatched chairs and tables served up fresh pastries, cakes, and hot drinks. Sophie waited for me there, head bent down over a book, steaming mug on the table in front of her. Absorbed in her reading, she didn't notice me until I had taken the seat opposite her. Her face lit up when she saw me.

"Hi, Sophie," I said cheerfully.

"Hello, Ms. Gibson." She beamed at me.

"Oh—since we're not in the classroom anymore, it's okay if you call me Chloe."

"Okay…*Chloe.*" She made a strange face as she said my name.

"And what do you prefer, Sungmi or Sophie?"

"I don't mind. You can keep calling me Sophie."

"Were you waiting long?"

"Not really. I came early just to have a look around the bookstore. This might be my favourite shop in all of Seoul."

I chuckled. "I love bookstores too. I didn't know about this one. Shall we get started?"

"Yes. I'm ready." She positioned a notebook in front of her and pulled a pen from her case.

I hadn't met Sophie's parents, but I had spoken to her mother on the phone. She didn't have any particular expectations for what I taught her, as long as I could help bring her language level up to what was required to study at an English university. This allowed me a lot of free rein over what to teach her. First, I wanted to assess Sophie's skill level more thoroughly, and I had devised an activity which would truly put her knowledge to the test. I pulled two books from my bag. One, a Korean novel, the other, an English translation of the same novel. I explained what I wanted her to do. "I'm going to choose a passage from the Korean book. I'd like you to try translating it to English as best you can, not word-for-word literally, but taking into account the nuances of the language. Once you've done that, we'll compare it to the professionally translated version."

Sophie's brow creased with concern. "Sounds difficult."

"That's the point. I don't expect you to be up to the level of a professional translator. Far from it. But it will show me your lapses in comprehension."

"Okay. I'll try my best."

I turned to the first bookmarked page where I had marked a section out in pencil. Sophie bit her lip in concentration as she pored over the passage. After reading it through twice, she slowly began to translate it in her notebook. I was very curious to see what she'd come up with.

Being the perfectionist she was, Sophie took her time, but at last she set down her pen. "Okay. I think I'm done. That was tough." She wiped the back of her hand across her forehead.

I opened the English version of the book where I had bookmarked the same passage. Sentence by sentence, we compared the two translations. This was when it became apparent that there were many gaps in her grasp of the language. Idioms, metaphors, and various other constructions were tripping her up.

I had her repeat the exercise once more using a different passage of text. Sophie tried even harder this time, and I allowed her to consult her Korean-English dictionary to help her. The result was the same. Her ability to translate was only surface level. She didn't understand the deeper intricacies of the language.

Disappointment reigned on Sophie's face. "Looks like I still have a lot to learn…"

"That's only natural—but your level is still outstanding for someone who has never lived in an English-speaking country," I said, trying to cheer her up.

For the rest of our allotted one-and-a-half-hour time slot, we simply conversed in English, and I would correct her every time she said something that didn't make sense. Eventually our conversation turned personal.

"Ms. Gibson—I mean, Chloe—can I ask you a personal question?" Sophie asked.

"Uh, okay. What do you want to know?"

"Do you have a boyfriend?"

My eyes widened in surprise at the sudden enquiry. "I... No. I don't." It was simpler just to say no.

"Oh."

"Why do you ask? Is there someone you like?"

Sophie's cheeks turned red. "Yes. But I don't know how to make him notice me."

I smiled, thinking she sounded just like a typical teenage girl. "You are a lovely person. Just be yourself and I'm sure he'll notice you."

She didn't look convinced. "But what if he's much more popular than I am?"

"All you can do is to try and be his friend and see if anything develops out of that."

"I see." She chewed her lip, absorbing my advice.

Checking my watch, I realised we had already gone well over the time limit of our session.

"Is the lesson over?" Sophie asked, frowning in disappointment.

"Yes. But I'm not in a hurry to do anything else. If you want to hang out a bit longer."

"I'd like that."

We browsed the bookstore together until evening.

———

"Maybe she has a crush on you," Yang Bora mused, finger to her chin.

"What? A crush on *me*?" I spluttered. "Don't be ridiculous." The very notion that Sophie might like me in that way seemed ludicrous.

Shin Jina looked equally surprised at Bora's conclusion.

We were seated around a table at Cinema Lumiere, chatting while we waited for the next film to start. Jina wasn't working, so she could watch it with us. I had come straight from Booksea, carrying a bag with my purchases. I told them how the tutoring session had gone and briefly mentioned Sophie's boy problems.

"Is it so ridiculous?" Bora asked. "You two seem to have grown quite an attachment."

I shook my head. "No. I don't think that's it. Surely not."

"She blushes around you, she gave you a gift, she asked you to be her personal tutor, and now she's confiding in you about her love life."

"That doesn't necessarily mean anything," Jina said, coming to my defence.

Bora pushed her glasses up the ridge of her nose. "Well, just sayin'. I'd be careful if I were you. It never pays for teachers to get too close to their students."

"True, but this is different," I said.

She cocked a brow. "How so? Because you're both female?"

"No..." Perhaps I had made a big mistake by talking too much about Sophie. I had given her the wrong impression.

"Proceed with caution, that's my advice. Keep things strictly professional."

"Hmmm. I'll keep that in mind."

The movie was about to begin, so we took our seats in the theatre. As the film played, I couldn't pay attention. My thoughts lingered on Bora's surprising analysis. Was I really too close with Sophie? Could our relationship be misconstrued? Was the boy Sophie had a crush on not actually a boy? Was it actually me? She did blush a lot in my presence, but that was the only thing which stood out. I tried to concentrate on the movie and block out the niggling feeling that Bora was actually right.

————

When I got home after the movie, I prepared a healthy home-cooked meal for dinner—a vegetable stir fry and rice. Since re-discovering cooking, I realised that I found the experience rather pleasant and relaxing.

After dinner, I sat on my bed with a hydrating sheet mask attached to my face, humming along to a catchy pop song while painting my toenails a vibrant shade of purple. My phone started ringing, interrupting my concentration, causing me to overrun my toenail and get nail polish on my duvet cover. I licked my finger and tried to rub it out which, unsurprisingly, didn't work. With my other hand I answered the phone without even looking at who was calling.

"Hey, it's me," Jinseung said.

I shot bolt upright at the sound of his voice. "Hey!"

"How's things?"

"Oh, you know, the usual. Actually, I'm tutoring one of my students privately now."

"Wow. That's great!"

"How's filming going? You sound tired."

He stifled a yawn. "It's progressing. I'm finally getting a break tomorrow. I plan to spend all day sleeping."

"Good plan."

"So, uh," he lowered his voice as if bringing up something secretive. "Have you had any more anonymous messages?"

"No. Not since you put up that letter to your fans. It seems to have done the trick. For now, at least."

He exhaled a sigh. "I'm relieved."

"Me too."

"Hey, your birthday is coming up soon, isn't it?"

"Yup. In two weeks."

"Keep the day free—no, the whole weekend. I want to arrange something."

My eyes widened. "Arrange what?"

"I can't tell you. That would spoil the surprise."

I overflowed with curiosity. "Come on, just tell me."

His firm answer was, "No."

"You're no fun," I muttered under my breath.

He abruptly changed the subject. "Hey, can you turn your camera on? I want to see you."

I did so, forgetting I still had the sheet mask on and the fluffy bunny headband holding my hair back.

Jinseung appeared on my screen too. He was sitting on a bed, propped up by a pile of pillows. His usual chubby cheeks were replaced by a gaunt and pallid visage, but dimples still appeared when he grinned upon seeing me.

I hastily peeled off the mask and removed the headband, cheeks blushing with embarrassment.

"Keep it on. I don't mind," he said, amused.

"I look silly."

"You look cute. But you always look cute."

I smiled sheepishly.

He was silent for a while, just gazing at me, his eyes drinking me in. Then he began to chew his lip in thought. "What have you got on under that robe?" he asked tentatively.

"Oh? My pyjamas."

"Can I see?"

I undid my waist tie and let the robe fall open. I wore a pair of classic blue plaid pyjamas. Comfortable and cute.

"Those are my favourite." He leaned back with an arm behind his head, admiring the view. "I haven't seen you in such a long time…Could you…?"

I knew what he was angling at. Despite my self-consciousness I decided to indulge him. I undid the first few of my buttons, revealing the plunging cleavage between my breasts.

He watched appreciatively. "Keep going," he breathed raggedly.

"I'm not wearing anything underneath."

"Show me."

I slowly undid the rest of my buttons. Jinseung watched on with a look of strained concentration.

When I got to the bottom, I edged my top open until my chest was fully exposed.

"You look so good."

"Now it's your turn."

"Is it just?"

I nodded.

He pulled off his black t-shirt in a swift motion. His physique was just as delicious as always, broad, toned, and hard. I wished I could reach through the screen and touch him. Jinseung displayed a similar look of yearning. "I wish you were here with me," he said.

"Me too."

That night, although separated by hundreds of kilometres, we regained some of our lost intimacy.

19

I received an unexpected visitor in my classroom one evening—Linda Choi, the principal/CEO of the *hagwon*. She was a middle-aged, half-Korean woman, short and slightly overweight, streaks of grey through her hair. She had a dour expression on her face. "Chloe, can I have a word with you after class?" she asked.

Her presence unnerved me, and I wondered what she wanted to speak with me about. "Yes, of course," I politely replied.

"Come to my office when you're ready."

I nodded and she left the room. Her request distracted my thoughts throughout the lesson. I couldn't help but jump to conclusions. Would she question my relationship with Sophie or, worst-case scenario, had she somehow found out about the private tutoring? She wasn't exactly a sympathetic woman, and she'd probably ask me to cease immediately or threaten to report me. Most likely I'd be let off with a warning first, but getting deported was a possible outcome I couldn't ignore.

I walked to Linda's office after class feeling extremely apprehensive. When I reached her door, I knocked before entering. The room reeked of her perfume—a sickly sweet artificial rose scent which made me gag. She sat behind a desk decorated with framed photographs of her cat—a hairless sphynx. I recoiled at the sight of the rat-like creature and tried to avert my eyes.

"Pull up a chair," Linda urged.

I sat down, fidgeting with my hands in my lap nervously.

"Kim Sungmi was in your class until recently, correct?" she asked, peering at me sternly through her spectacles.

I gulped. "Yes, that's right."

"You don't happen to have her contact details, do you?"

I hesitated. Was this a trap? Was she trying to find out if I'd been in touch with Sophie since she left? "No," I lied.

She tapped her nails on the desk, sighing. "That's too bad."

"Do you need to contact her?"

"Yes." She leaned closer to me and lowered her spectacles. "Kim Sungmi may have left us, but it doesn't excuse her from paying the term's fee. Her tuition is well overdue. I have been trying to contact her parents to recoup the outstanding payment, but I can't seem to get through to anyone."

So that's what this is about. I felt a mixture of relief for myself and concern for Sophie. It seemed strange that her parents were capable of paying a private tutor but not her overdue *hagwon* fees.

"Well, never mind," Linda said relaxing back into her chair. "I'll just have to switch tactics. Perhaps I'll get a debt collector involved at some point…"

A debt collector! I made a mental note to warn Sophie or her parents.

"You may go home," Linda said with a gentle shooing gesture of her hand.

"Sorry I wasn't of any help."

"That's okay. Enjoy your evening."

"Goodnight, Linda."

I had no further work to do that night, so I left straight away and walked to the bus stop. Usually, I had my transit card ready before I boarded, but I wasn't thinking straight. I held up the queue while I fumbled in my bag searching for it. At last I gripped the card at the bottom of my bag. When I retrieved it, something else fluttered out and onto the floor of the bus. Before I could react, someone behind me picked it up. "You dropped this."

"Thanks." I accepted the small piece of crumpled light pink paper, though I didn't recall what it was.

Curious, I unfolded the piece of paper once I sat down. It was a note, and as soon as I read it, a loud gasp escaped my throat.

LAST CHANCE. BREAK UP WITH SHIN JINSEUNG OR ELSE YOU'LL PAY.

The *ajumma* next to me turned my way, alarmed by my sudden outburst. "Are you okay?"

"Yes," I said quickly, recovering my breath. "I'm fine."

I stuffed the note back into my bag, hands trembling. My thoughts were a scrambled mess, but as soon as I had calmed down, I tried to think through the situation rationally. *What does this mean?* The stalker must have been in close proximity with me at some point—close enough to slip a note in my bag undetected.

How long had it been there? Maybe it had been put there a while ago and I didn't notice until now—its crumpled appearance certainly suggested that it wasn't new, and I didn't regularly empty out my bag, letting the receipts and other miscellanea build up instead.

"OR ELSE YOU'LL PAY." *How will I pay? Am I in danger? Would the police take this seriously or not?*

Caught up in these thoughts, I nearly missed my stop. The door had already closed, but I called to the driver and he opened it again to let me off.

Alone at the bus stop, a cold wind swirled around me, making the hairs on my exposed neck stand up. I cautiously walked the short distance home, constantly glancing around, making sure no one followed me.

I slumped with a sense of relief when I reached my apartment building unscathed. The stalker might have known where I lived, but I still had faith in the security of my building.

I entered my code and pushed open the door to my apartment. It quickly dawned on me that I wasn't alone.

20

———

I dropped my bag in shock. Its contents scattered over the floor. A woman I didn't recognise stood in the middle of my apartment. She was young and pretty with long dark hair and glass-like skin. She had an innocent look except for a pair of shrewd eyes which were piercing in their intensity.

"Who are you?" I stammered.

The young woman just stared at me for a bit, then her lip slowly curled up at one corner. She started to approach me. I impulsively backed away.

"Are you all right?" she asked as if I were the strange person and not her.

"What are you doing in my apartment?"

The woman raised her perfectly groomed eyebrows. "Didn't Manager Yang tell you?"

"Yang Bora?" *What does she have to do with all this?*

I heard the toilet flush, the sound of running water, then Bora emerged from the bathroom. "Oh! Hello, Chloe. You're home."

"What are you doing here?" I asked.

"Didn't you get my message? I tried calling you as well, but you didn't answer."

"Who is this?" I pointed to the young woman accusingly.

"Don't you recognise her? It's Go Yoojin."

I calmed myself, breathing slow and steady. It was only the actor who Bora managed. If I wasn't completely flabbergasted, I'd be starstruck. "Why did you bring her here?"

"There's a ghost in my apartment," Yoojin said simply.

A ghost? This makes no sense. Am I dreaming?

"Actor-nim is very superstitious," Bora explained. "She refused to go to her apartment. I didn't know what else to do so I brought her here in the meantime. Sorry you didn't see my message. It must have been a shock."

"Shock is an understatement."

"I'm sorry."

"How did you get in?"

"You gave me your door code for safekeeping, remember?"

"Oh yeah."

In fact, I had let Bora go to my apartment when I wasn't there a few times in the past, so it was no wonder she thought it would be all right this time.

"Speaking of ghosts, it looks like *you've* seen one," Bora said, eyeing me with concern.

"I thought…"

"What?"

"I thought that my stalker had gained entrance. I found this in my bag just before." I took out the note and showed Bora.

"*Omo!*" She clutched a hand to her chest. "That's serious."

Yoojin caught a peek at the note as well. "Yikes! Are you dating *Seonbae*?"

"Yes," I admitted, too depleted to come up with a convincing lie. "But it's a secret, okay?"

"I won't tell anyone."

"You need to sit down." Bora guided me to the couch. "I'll get you a glass of water and clean up the stuff you dropped."

I slumped down, my heart still pounding on overdrive. My hand shook as I drank the water.

When Bora had finished picking up my things, she sat down next to me. "Do you think…you could be in danger?" she asked, a slight tremor in her voice.

"I did think so when I read the note. But then again, I don't know when it ended up in my bag. It could've been days or weeks ago. I thought that Jinseung's announcement had worked, and I'd just been going about totally carefree. Obviously nothing happened to me."

"Perhaps they're just trying to scare you and don't actually intend to 'make you pay'?"

"Yes. That's a possibility…But I'm still scared."

"I think you should get the police involved. Better to be safe than sorry."

"I'm worried they won't take this seriously."

"Maybe so, but it's worth it just to bring it to their attention."

"Yeah, you're right. It couldn't hurt to try and explain the situation. Maybe there's something they can do."

Yoojin had been hovering around us listening in on our conversation. "Is this person a fan of Shin Jinseung?" she piped up.

"That's what we suspect," Bora said.

Yoojin stroked her chin in thought. "How strange. Usually, the goal of *sasaeng* fans is to get noticed by their idol, but this person seems to be hiding in the shadows."

Bora contemplated this. "True, but at the moment it seems

their only aim is to get Chloe and Jinseung to break up. Perhaps he or she plans to 'come out of the shadows' once they've broken up?"

"I don't know. Something seems off about this…"

"I don't disagree, but it's impossible to try and guess their exact motive right now. Best put this in the hands of the police. Chloe, I'll go with you to the station if you want."

"Oh? That would be a big help," I said, grateful for her support.

Bora turned her attention to Yoojin. "Actor-nim, I better take you home…"

Yoojin crossed her arms and shook her head. "No way. I'm not going home until it has been thoroughly cleansed of ghosts."

"The paranormal agent can't come until tomorrow, and you can't stay here. I'll book you into a hotel tonight, would that suit?"

"Make it the Four Seasons and you have a deal."

Bora let out an exasperated sigh. "Mr. Kim won't like this one bit…"

Yoojin looked at her with puppy-dog eyes.

"Fine. I'll make a booking." She grabbed her iPad off the dining table and started tapping away. At the payment screen, she whipped out a platinum business credit card and typed in the details. "There. All done. Let's go. Chloe, you're coming too."

"I am?"

"Once I've dropped Yoojin off, I'll take you to the police station."

Before leaving, I quickly saved my electronic file of evidence onto a flash drive. I also grabbed the pieces of phys- ical evidence I had and stowed them safely in my bag.

We left the apartment. Yoojin covered the lower half of her

face with a surgical mask and pulled a hood over her head to disguise herself as we walked the short distance to where the van was parked.

I took the passenger seat next to Bora, while Yoojin climbed in the back. My muscles tensed as Bora started the engine. Past experience of Bora's driving taught me not to get too relaxed. Fortunately, her driving seemed to have improved a great deal. We made it to the hotel without incident.

"You okay to check in by yourself?" Bora asked Yoojin when she had stopped outside the main entrance. "I booked you under the pseudonym Do Minha."

"Sure. Hope you get along okay at the police station."

"Thanks," I said.

Yoojin disappeared into the luxurious hotel through the revolving door.

"Right. Off to the police station," Bora said, pulling away from the hotel.

"Wait. We need to make a stopover somewhere."

She looked at me questioningly.

"There's more evidence I should bring with me," I explained.

"Oh right. The doll."

"Yes. And the other note."

"There's another note?"

"Jinseung was holding back from me. It turned out that there was a similar note with the doll."

"It certainly would have been handy to know that before."

"You're telling me."

"Okay. Let's go to Jinseung's place."

We drove to his apartment building. Bora parked nearby and I ran out, up the elevator, and into his apartment, praying that the evidence was still there and he hadn't given it to Changsoo like he said he would.

All was quiet and still. The air smelled faintly of cleaning detergent, which told me that his cleaner must have recently been in to freshen up the place.

Now, where did he say he kept the doll? In a drawer? It couldn't be a drawer in the bedroom, closet, or en suite, as I had waited on his bed while he put the doll away.

That left the kitchen or his office room, and I doubted that he kept it in the kitchen so close to where he prepared food. The office was the most likely contender. There were few drawers in the small room—just a small set inside a cupboard, and his desk drawers. I searched his desk first, pulling out each drawer one by one until I got to the bottom. Most were filled with random papers and folders, but the last drawer contained what I was looking for. The doll, sealed in a plastic bag, along with the note: "BREAK UP WITH CHLOE GIBSON."

I grabbed what I had come for and rushed back down to Bora's van.

"Did you find it?" she asked.

I nodded.

"Good. The more evidence we have, the better, and that doll is quite compelling."

As she drove me to the police station, my stomach clenched with nervousness. What if the police couldn't do anything to help me? What if they thought I was making things up? Thank goodness Bora was with me for support. I didn't think I'd be able to do this on my own.

We pulled up in the carpark outside the police station—a large, generic-looking office building with a flat blue roof. Flags fluttered in the wind above the entryway. Bora and I walked side by side up the steps to the main door. Cold, harsh fluorescent lights lit the reception area. Bora explained my situation to the person at the desk. The receptionist handed me a clipboard with a blank police report attached. She asked me to fill out the report while I waited to be called up, then we would be referred to an officer we could speak to.

An eclectic group of individuals milled around the waiting area. Bora and I sat down on hard plastic seats. An old man wearing dirty, tatty clothes leered at me in a way that made my skin crawl. I would have felt unsafe if we weren't inside a police station.

The hours dragged on. People came and went from the station. I had already filled out the report and checked it over twice, making sure I hadn't left out any important details. Bora took it up to the receptionist.

I had almost nodded off to sleep in my chair by the time my name was finally called. Bora gently shook my shoulder, making sure I was awake. "Chloe? We're up."

A staff member took us through a door to an open-plan office area where police staff were stationed at desks around the room. We were guided to a young man. He had defined cheekbones and closely shaved hair. The bulging biceps visible below his rolled-up shirt sleeves announced his athletic body. He couldn't have been older than thirty.

"Good evening, I'm Officer Bae Sangwook," he said. "I have had a brief read of your report, but could you explain everything to me from the beginning?"

I was silent for a moment, unable to process my thoughts into a coherent sentence. Bora nudged me. "The doll," she mouthed.

"Right." I explained everything starting from the doll incident.

All the while, Sangwook listened intently, taking notes

while I spoke. I covered everything that had happened up to the discovery of the note in my bag. I also handed him the flash drive, the physical notes, and the doll. Sangwook perused the evidence. To my relief, he appeared to be taking everything very seriously.

"You were right to report this," Officer Bae said.

His reassurance instantly soothed me.

"However…" he continued.

My heart plunged. I already knew what was coming next.

"…I'm afraid a case like this is low priority. There has been no concrete threat of physical harm. From what I can tell, you aren't in any immediate danger. Your situation must be stressful, I'll give you that, but stress is not enough to start a police investigation. I will, of course, open a case file, though."

"What about a DNA test?" I asked.

"We would need a suspect's DNA to run a comparison."

"Then what should we do, Officer-nim?" Bora asked, frowning.

"Keep gathering proof and send it to me. The culprit could slip up at one point and reveal something about their identity. Once we have something to go on, maybe then we'll be able to do something. And if at any point, you feel physically threatened, contact me immediately."

He gave us each a copy of his card which listed his contact details.

We went back to the car, a sombre mood hanging over us.

"I knew it. They won't investigate," I grumbled, pulling on my seatbelt.

"It wasn't all for nothing," Bora said.

"Oh?"

She waved Bae Sangwook's business card. "We have

someone who we can contact now. Who knows when this could come in handy."

"That's true. But still, I feel like a sitting duck."

"Don't worry. I'll keep in touch with you and help you with whatever I can."

"Thanks. I appreciate that."

21

As I approached Sophie in the bookshop café, Bora's warning replayed in my head. "I'd be careful if I were you. It never pays for teachers to get too close to their students." While I still didn't believe there was anything wrong with my friendship with Sophie, I made a mental note to keep things professional during our session.

The café was pleasantly quiet with only a few solo patrons present, calmly sipping drinks while reading books or working on laptops. Sophie sat at a small table by the window, carefully writing in a notebook, a look of deep concentration etched on her face. She was casually dressed in jeans and an oversized sweater. I pulled out the chair opposite her. "Hello," I said, sitting myself down.

Sophie closed her notebook. The smile on her lips faded as she examined me. "Are you okay?"

"I'm fine, thank you."

"You look out of sorts."

"Oh? I guess I'm just a bit tired." Exhausted, more like. The stalking and the police's unwillingness to investigate weighed heavily on me, but I wasn't about to go into that with Sophie. She didn't seem convinced, but she didn't press the matter.

As I prepared my teaching materials, a niggling feeling developed in the back of my mind. There was something I had to tell Sophie about, but I couldn't remember what. No matter how hard I tried to grasp the memory, it kept slipping away. I had no choice but to let it go and move on.

I took out my phone to set a timer. "I'm going to time today's lesson," I explained. "Hope you don't mind."

"No, go ahead."

I was about to press start when she stopped me.

"Wait. I'm going to go get another drink. Want anything?"

"Ah, no thanks."

She went to the counter. When I saw her open her wallet to pay, it hit me. The debt collector. I had called Sophie's mother not long after my meeting with Linda, but I hadn't been able to get through to her, and with everything that had been going on, it had completely slipped my mind. When she rejoined me at the table, I didn't hesitate to bring it up. "Sophie, there's something I need to warn you about."

Her eyes widened. "What's that?"

"I had a chat with the principal of the *hagwon* a few days ago. She told me that your fees haven't been paid and she's been unable to get hold of your family. She was seriously considering hiring a debt collector."

The news appeared to throw her off-guard. She seemed flustered, unable to hold eye contact with me. "Thank you for warning me."

I had intended to keep my distance from her, but in this situation, I couldn't help getting personal. If Sophie was in some kind of trouble, I wanted to help her. "Sorry to pry, but is everything all right? Is your family having any financial difficulties?"

She shook her head and summoned up a smile. "No. Don't worry. I'm not sure why my parents haven't paid. They're very busy and they must have forgotten. I'll remind them."

"Okay. But just so you know, you can tell me if anything's wrong."

"Thanks."

———

When the timer went off, I wondered if I had set it wrong since it felt like hardly any time had passed at all. But no, one and a half hours had really gone by and our lesson was over. "Looks like our time's up," I said regretfully.

Sophie frowned. "That went quick."

"I know. Must have achieved a flow state."

"Flow state?"

"When you're so involved in what you're doing that time just flies by."

"Oh, I get it. That happens to me all the time."

"It means you have a great deal of focus. No wonder you're such a good student."

Sophie's cheeks glowed red. "It doesn't usually happen during a lesson, though. Must be your teaching."

I chuckled. "Maybe, but I can't take all the credit. Let's finish up now."

We quickly wrapped up the activity we were engaged in.

Sophie packed her notebook and pens away. "Do you want to have a look around the bookshop again?" she asked hopefully.

I was tempted but thought better of it. "No, I need to head home."

"Oh. Okay." She drooped in disappointment.

"But don't let me stop you from browsing."

"Nah. That's okay. I'll head home too. Why don't we walk together? Part of the way, anyway. It's nice weather."

Since the latest threatening note, I hadn't been walking around by myself very much. I had planned to take a taxi home, but if Sophie was offering to walk with me, then perhaps it wouldn't hurt if I went with her. It seemed safer than going alone. "All right," I agreed. "Let's walk."

We set out. The evening was warm and still. Birds twittered in blossoming trees. The sky was pink as the sun descended below the horizon. I kept an anxious eye out as we walked. Sophie called out my odd behaviour. "Something wrong?"

"No. It's nothing."

Eventually, I relaxed. We chatted as we walked, discussing the latest English books that Sophie had read.

Further into our journey, our chitchat began to peter out. Sophie seemed a bit distracted, constantly checking her phone. I wondered who she was texting. We turned onto a quiet backstreet with an office building along one side, and the rear side of a strip of shops on the other. The last remnants of sunlight were beginning to fade, plunging the street into shadow. Our pace slowed. I heard something from above—the swish of an opening window. Sophie let out a scream. It all happened so fast that my brain didn't register what was going on.

22

An object whooshed past me, missing me by mere centimetres. It shattered loudly on the concrete, sending shards of glass flying at every angle. I sprang out of the way, heart thumping wildly in my chest.

"Are you all right?" Sophie asked, eyes wide with shock.

I brushed myself off. "Yes. It missed me. Just."

A man came running from a nearby shop, startled by the noise. "What happened?" he asked.

Neither Sophie nor I replied, too shaken by the event. Once I had caught my breath I looked up. All the windows were shut, and I couldn't see anyone there. Whoever did it would have run away by now.

"What is that, anyway?" Sophie asked.

I bent down to inspect the remains of the object. "Looks like a vase."

"Someone threw that at you?" the man asked, bewildered.

"They dropped it from that window," I said, pointing up.

He held up a hand to his mouth and gasped. "*Omo*. Who would do such a thing?"

"I don't know," I replied.

"A random attack?" Sophie suggested.

"There are crazy, dangerous people out there," the man said, shaking his head. "Are you okay?"

"Yes, I think so." I examined and flexed my limbs. If I had been hurt, the adrenaline coursing through me covered up the pain.

The man took a notepad from his pocket and scribbled something down. He tore off a page and handed it to me. "Here," he said. "My contact details in case you need a witness. You will report this, won't you?"

"Yes. I'll report it."

"I'll check the shop's CCTV footage in case it shows anything useful."

"That would be a big help."

"I'll clean up this mess too. Don't want anyone to hurt themselves."

"Thank you, *Ajussi*," Sophie said.

"You better leave. The attacker might still be lurking around somewhere."

"Yes, we'll go," I said. "Thanks again."

"That was scary," Sophie admitted as we left the scene.

I didn't share with her what I was thinking—that it wasn't just some random attack. That perhaps I was intentionally targeted. The stalker warned me that I'd pay, and maybe that vase wasn't meant to miss me.

———

As soon as I was home safe and sound, I pulled out Officer Bae Sangwook's card from my wallet. I called him to report the incident. The line was busy at first, but I tried again a bit later and managed to get through.

"Officer Bae Sangwook speaking," he said.

"Hello, this is Chloe Gibson. I saw you at the police station a few days ago. I reported being harassed by someone trying to break up my relationship."

"Ah, yes. I remember. Is everything okay?"

I explained to him what had just occurred and my strong suspicion that the attacker was the same person who had been sending me the notes.

"Are you completely sure about that?" Sangwook asked.

"I can't be one hundred per cent sure, but that's the way it seems. They warned me I'd pay, and then this happens."

"Hmmm…"

"You're not convinced?"

"How could they position themselves to drop the vase without knowing in advance that you would walk by that exact building?"

"Must have been following me, or tracking me somehow, and saw me turn onto that street."

"It would have been difficult to get into the building and up several floors in time."

"True…" Now that he said that, it did seem like a stretch. Doubt edged its way into my mind.

"Is it not possible that this was, after all, a random attack? Unrelated to the messages?"

"It's possible," I admitted.

"Rest assured, we will investigate this. You could have been seriously injured, or worse, killed."

"Thank you. Oh—there were witnesses too." I gave him the phone numbers of Sophie and the man from the shop—Lee Haneul.

"That's helpful. Be careful, okay? Give me a call if anything else happens."

"Yes. I will."

The next person I called was Yang Bora.

"That's really scary, Chloe," she said. "I hope you're all right."

"Officer Bae doesn't think it's the same person. But it seems like too much of a coincidence if it's not."

"I agree with you."

"I don't know what to do."

"I've been thinking about your situation lately, and I think I've come up with a plan."

"Oh? What is it?"

"I don't know why I didn't think of it before. You don't need to break up with Jinseung, you just need to make the stalker believe that you have."

"And how would I manage that?"

"You and Shin Jinseung are actors. Time to put those acting skills to use and stage a breakup scene."

"A breakup scene? Interesting…"

"And if we play our cards right, we might just be able to catch the stalker at the same time."

23

Chloe: I will break up with Shin Jinseung.

My finger hovered over the send button, hand shaking. Is this the right thing to do? Will it work? I wasn't even sure if they would be able to reply. I hadn't received a text from the stalker in a while, and I was relying on them receiving my message at the last number they contacted me on.

I held my breath, and before I could talk myself out of it, I hit send. This was my best shot at ending the torment I had been going through once and for all.

I waited for the status of my message to turn to "read." To my surprise, it happened quickly, then three dots in the bottom corner showed that the recipient was typing. Their message popped up with a ping.

Unknown: How will you prove it?

I quickly typed my answer.

Chloe: Meet me and I will make a call to break up with him.

I gritted my teeth and waited for the reply.

Unknown: I will not meet you face to face, but make the call somewhere I can see you.

Fortunately, I had anticipated such a response.

Chloe: How about a coffee shop? You can watch from a distance.
Unknown: I need to hear the call too. There is an app that will let me listen in. I will send you a link to download it.

I wondered why watching would be necessary if they could simply listen to the call from any location.

Chloe: You need to see me and listen in as well?
Unknown: Yes. I need to get a good sense that the call is genuine. I will watch you and listen. That's the only way I'll believe you.

So they were already suspicious that the call might be fake. This could be trickier to pull off than I had anticipated. Plus, downloading something that the stalker sent me seemed seriously risky, but what choice did I have?

Chloe: Fine. Let's do as you say.
Unknown: You better go through with it.

———

Bora and I had named our plan "Operation Breakup," and it was finally time to put it into action.

The coffee shop bustled with late-morning patrons. It was much busier than I had anticipated. As I stood in line to purchase a drink, I scanned the large room, trying to identify anyone who looked suspicious. The clientele was varied— businesspeople in suits, casually dressed creative types, and university students. No one in particular stood out, but I knew that my stalker, my *enemy*, must be among them. I tried not to think about it too much.

"What would you like?" the staff member behind the counter asked.

I had been so preoccupied I didn't notice that I was at the front of the queue. "I'll have a white chocolate mocha, please." I wanted something sweet to sip to keep me going through the arduous task ahead.

After a short wait, I picked up my coffee and sat down at a small table in the centre of the room. I had downloaded the app on my phone which would allow the stalker to listen in on the call at 11:00 am. I checked the time. 10:57 am. My whole body was tense with anticipation. Could I really pull this off? Could I make this breakup look realistic enough to be convincing?

I kept checking the time, but it seemed frozen. Finally, the clock ticked over from 10:59 to 11:00. I cleared my throat, took a deep breath, then I called him.

"Hi, Chloe. What did you want to talk about?" Jinseung answered, a note of apprehension in his voice.

He was in on the act, I reminded myself.

"*Oppa*...there's something I have to tell you."

He took a sharp intake of breath. "What's wrong? Has something happened?"

"I...I..."

"I'm listening. Tell me what's the matter."

I paused, gathering my words. "This might come as a shock, but...I think we should break up."

The line went silent for a moment. "Are you serious?" He sounded bewildered and upset.

"Yes. I'm serious."

"I don't understand...Why? Why would you do this to me?"

Although we were only acting, the agony in his voice was difficult to listen to. I continued on, explaining my situation. "I think I'll be in danger if I keep on seeing you. That stalker...it's all getting too much for me to bear. I can't keep doing this. I can't go on."

"There must be some other way to work this out...I'll think of something, I swear I will."

"No. I'm afraid this is the only way. We have to break up. I'm so sorry."

"But—"

"Please don't try to contact me again."

"Wait—"

I ended the call, feeling overwhelmed with emotion. Tears welled up in my eyes. I didn't realise that a fake breakup could be so genuinely heartbreaking. On the plus side, looking miserable helped my act.

Several people in the coffee shop stared at me, and I felt painfully self-conscious. Wiping tears from my eyes with my sweater sleeve, I quickly deleted the spying app from my phone, then got up and left without finishing my drink.

In the public bathroom of the subway station, I cleaned my face with a wipe and reapplied my makeup. *Deep breaths*, I told myself, looking at my reflection in the dirty mirror. My heart was still racing. *I've done my part. Now all I have to do is wait.*

Unable to sit still, I paced up and down the length of the waiting area with my phone clutched tightly in my hand in case Bora or Sangwook tried to contact me. My mind reeled with possible outcomes and I felt so nervous I could be sick.

"Chloe!" came a voice across the station. Yang Bora rushed towards me. I ran to her and we met in the middle by the ticket vending machines.

"What is it? What happened?" I asked, grasping her by the shoulders.

She grinned. "The operation has been a success. The stalker has been caught."

———

My role in the operation was probably the easiest part. Yang Bora and Officer Bae Sangwook had the hard job. While I staged the breakup, Bora and Sangwook were watching, trying to identify the stalker.

Bora explained that Bae Sangwook had indeed spotted someone acting suspiciously. "After you left, Officer Bae showed him his police badge and asked him whether he had been listening in on a call. He denied it at first, but when asked to see his phone he confessed."

"What happened? Where is he now?"

"Officer Bae took him to the police station for further questioning."

"Has he been arrested?"

"No. I don't think so."

"What did he look like? Has he admitted to the stalking? Gosh. I have so many questions..."

"He was young and kinda dorky-looking. Skinny, tall, and wearing glasses. I don't know much more than what I've already told you. Let's go to the police station. I'm sure we can find out more."

"All right. Let's go."

We rushed up the steps out of the subway exit and hailed a taxi. I twitched with impatience in the back seat as we travelled at a snail's pace in the traffic. All the while, I kept my eyes glued to my phone in case Sangwook contacted me.

"No need to fret," Bora said. "The interview will probably take a while. I'm sure we won't miss anything."

Her words of reassurance did little to calm me down. I was anxious for the whole ride.

When the police station eventually came into view, we were still stuck behind a queue of cars.

"Driver, we'll get out now," Bora said. "It'll be faster to walk from here."

I handed him some cash and we hopped out in the standstill traffic.

"Nearly there," Bora said, as we dodged pedestrians on the footpath.

Through the gate, the carpark, then up the steps, we arrived at the entryway, Korean flags flapping overhead. It hadn't been all that long since our last visit to this police station, but everything looked somehow different in daylight.

Bora spoke to reception. "Could you please let Officer Bae Sangwook know that Yang Bora and Chloe Gibson are here?"

"Sure, please take a seat." The receptionist gestured to the waiting area.

We sat down at the row of chairs by the window. Apart from an elderly couple, we were the only ones there. I fidgeted, rocking my heels back and forth on the floor as we waited.

"I'm sure everything will go fine," Bora said. "The police already have all the evidence."

"But what happens next? What if I'm asked if I want to press charges? Will I need a lawyer?"

"Don't get too ahead of yourself. I'm sure Officer Bae will explain what you need to do."

"I'm so nervous."

"Just think, all this stalking business will be over soon, and your life can return to normal."

"I hope so."

The elderly couple were called in before we were. Bora got up and poured us each a cup of cold water from the dispenser in the corner.

"I wonder what's taking so long?" I asked as she passed me a cup.

"I'm sure they have to be very thorough with their questioning."

Just then, someone emerged from the office door. I stood up in reaction, expecting it to be Bae Sangwook, but it wasn't him. It was a lanky guy, maybe a few years older than me. He had floppy black hair and wore silver wire-framed glasses. He matched Bora's description. I froze, staring at him in shock. *That's him. He's my stalker.* He glanced back at me with an inscrutable expression. It looked like he was about to say something, but he shrugged it off and walked straight to the exit.

"What's going on?" I asked Bora. "Why did he get set free just like that?"

"I have no idea." She looked just as confused as I was.

Bae Sangwook entered the room.

"Officer Bae!" I cried. "What happened?"

"Come through and I'll explain." He ushered us to the office.

My legs were shaking as I took a seat opposite him. "Who was that man? Why did you let him go?"

Sangwook scratched his head. "Your stalker is much smarter than we anticipated."

"So…it wasn't him?"

"Unfortunately not."

"Then who was he?"

"A journalist."

"What?"

"Your stalker didn't come. He or she tipped off a journalist instead."

Bora's expression morphed into a look of dawning comprehension. "Oh, that *is* smart."

"I don't get it!" I said. My brain was too frazzled to make sense of anything.

"Rather than going there and risking being exposed, they sent a journalist," she explained. "The stalker would get confirmation that the breakup happened, and the journalist would get something juicy to publish in return."

"That's right," Sangwook said.

"Then does the journalist know who the stalker is?" I asked.

"Unfortunately not. The tip-off was sent anonymously through an encrypted email service."

"Damn. Does that mean we're no closer to catching them?"

"Not necessarily. I asked Yeo Chul—the journalist—to continue contacting them via email to try and wheedle out more information. He will pretend that everything went smoothly and that an article about the breakup will be published."

"There won't really be an article, will there?" Bora asked, a hint of panic in her voice.

"Don't worry. I made him delete his recording of the phone call, and he swore he wouldn't publish anything."

"Phew."

I drooped in my seat, still in the process of absorbing everything. *So, we didn't catch the stalker after all, but at least the fake breakup part was a success.*

"Thanks for everything, Officer Bae," Bora said. "Our plan wasn't as foolproof as we thought, but thank you so much for helping us go through with it."

"I don't usually get involved in harebrained schemes like this, you know. I only helped because I thought you'd try to catch them on your own otherwise."

"Well, you're right about that."

Sangwook chuckled. "I'll be in contact with Yeo Chul about the emails and I'll let you know if I find anything else out."

Bora and I thanked him again before leaving. We walked side by side to the subway station, the afternoon sun glowing faintly through a gap between skyscrapers.

"We didn't catch the stalker after all," I said, head bowed in disappointment.

"It wasn't all for nothing," Bora said. "We have Yeo Chul on our side now, and the stalker must think you've broken up with Jinseung. Hopefully, they'll stop harassing you, but be careful, okay?"

"Huh?"

"I'm just saying not to let your guard down too much. If they manage to work out that you didn't really break up, then you'll be back at square one."

"Yes. You're right. I didn't think about that."

"Best play it safe. Keep contact with Jinseung to a minimum until you're sure the stalking has stopped."

I let out an exasperated sigh. "And here I was thinking that my life would return to normal…So much for that."

24

I cringed in embarrassment as Yang Bora sang at the top of her lungs outside my door. The whole floor of apartments could no doubt hear her off-key rendition of the Happy Birthday song. "Happy Birthday to yooouuuuuu!" she bellowed. "Happy Birthday to yoouuuu! Happy birthday dear Chloeeeee. Happy Birthday to you!"

"Shhhh! Come inside," I beckoned.

Bora stepped into my apartment and produced the object she held behind her back—a present wrapped in shiny purple paper with a pink ribbon attached. "Open it," she urged, thrusting it at me.

I gratefully accepted the gift, giving it a little shake to see if I could determine what was inside.

"Don't do that!" Bora said. "Just open it."

I began the painstaking task of unwrapping the gift, trying not to damage the beautiful paper. "What is it?" I asked, still in the process of unwrapping.

"Wait and see."

"The anticipation is killing me." I managed to slide the wrapping off, revealing a lidded black box.

"Go on. Open the box."

I carefully removed the lid. A pair of pretty silver ballet flats lay nestled in white tissue paper inside. I ran an appreciative hand over the dainty shoes. They were just my style.

"Do you like them?" Bora asked.

"They're so cute! Thank you!" I slipped them on, trying them for size. "Perfect!"

After gushing over the shoes a while, I put them back in their box and added it to the pile of gifts I had accumulated on the table: A beautiful handmade wooden jewellery box from my parents, a set of Amore Pacific skincare products from Shin Jina, a small bottle of Givenchy perfume from Han Seri, and a box of loose-leaf teas—each one with a different healing property—from my host parents in Tongyeong. Even Seo Minjung had sent me a card with a heartfelt birthday message inside. Too bad the one person whom I most wanted to acknowledge my birthday hadn't done anything at all.

"What did you get from Jinseung?" Bora asked.

"Ah…well…" I twiddled my fingers.

"I bet it was something really expensive."

I shook my head, eyes downcast. "Actually, he hasn't given me anything."

Her mouth dropped open in outrage. "What?"

"And I haven't heard from him at all today."

"I know you guys have been keeping your distance because of the whole fake breakup and stalker thing, but surely he could have found a way to celebrate your birthday in secret."

"He told me to keep the weekend free, but it seems like he's forgotten."

Bora tightened her hands into fists. "That jerk! I'll call him and give him a piece of my mind."

"No! I mean, I'd rather give him the benefit of the doubt. There's still the rest of the day."

"You're much more tolerant of this than I would be."

"Yeah, well, I have to exercise a great deal of patience in this relationship."

"I sure hope he comes through with something."

"Me too."

Bora squeezed my shoulder. "Anyway, I've got to go. I have appointments I need to attend with Go Yoojin. Sorry I can't stay."

"That's all right."

"Hope your birthday improves! I'll organise a party for you another day if it doesn't."

"I might just hold you to that. Thanks again for the shoes!"

Bora left humming the Happy Birthday tune. It was too bad she couldn't stay. I really could have done with some company.

Hours passed with no word from Jinseung. I should have been out celebrating, not moping around the house all day.

As night fell, I came to terms with the fact that he had forgotten me, or was otherwise too busy to even wish me a happy birthday. I dropped to the couch with a sigh, holding my head in my hands. *I can't believe this.* Since we made up after our fight, I thought things had improved between us. Obviously I was wrong. *He doesn't care much about me after all…*

Before I could stop myself, I was at the pantry searching for junk food to consume. I had been good for so long, preparing healthy meals and refraining from too much sugar and salt, but this latest injustice had pushed me to my limit.

I rummaged the shelves in a frenzy, but since I had stopped buying junk food a while ago, there was nothing unhealthy to be found. I decided to walk to the convenience store and buy something.

Outside the building, I was greeted by the view of flower petals blowing across the footpath in the wind. A discarded bouquet lay on the ground, all messed up and trampled upon. *How sad.* I wondered how it got there. I was about to reach down to look at the attached notecard but thought better of it. It was dirty and probably illegible at this point.

Leaving the ruined flowers behind without a second thought, I walked to the convenience store. A bell sounded upon my entrance. Row after row of bright and colourfully packaged goods stood out beneath stark white lighting. I traipsed through the aisles, loading up my arms with junk food until I couldn't carry any more.

As I approached the counter with my extra-large haul, a deep sense of shame descended upon me. *I shouldn't be doing this. I've come too far to undo all of my hard work now.* Weighed down with guilt, I slowed to a halt then turned around, making up my mind to put everything back bar one small treat—it was my birthday, after all.

On the way back up to my apartment, my phone started to ring. I immediately stopped in my tracks to answer it, thinking the caller was Jinseung. But it wasn't Jinseung who answered. It was a male voice I didn't recognise. "Ms. Chloe Gibson?"

"Yes?" I answered, bemused.

"Your taxi has arrived."

Huh? I never ordered a taxi…"Sorry?"

"The taxi is waiting at the entrance."

"There must be some mistake…"

"The booking was made by a Mr. Shin. Does that sound correct?"

Jinseung booked it for me? Why hasn't he told me anything? "Oh…okay. I'll be down in a minute." *What's this all about?*

25

The classy black limo awaiting me gleamed luxuriously under the streetlight. A driver stood by the door wearing a dark suit and driving gloves. I tentatively approached, bewildered by this strange turn of events.

"Good evening, Ms. Gibson." The driver bowed politely then opened the door for me.

I stared at the empty back seat before hesitantly climbing in. The sleek interior smelled of freshly cleaned leather. Before pulling on my seatbelt I leaned forward to ask the driver a question. "Excuse me, but, where are we going?"

"Gimpo Airport," he replied, adjusting the rear-view mirror.

"*Omo!*"

"The booking indicated that you have a flight to Jeju Island at nine o'clock this evening."

"Oh! I see."

"Is everything okay, Ms. Gibson? Gimpo is correct, is it not?"

"Yes. Thank you."

So, I was going to Jeju Island. To think I ever doubted Jinseung. He had planned the best birthday present ever—I would get to see him again. The only downside was that I had nothing with me apart from my wallet, phone, and keys, and the chocolate I had bought from the convenience store. I wasn't wearing nice clothes or any makeup. The trip was a wonderful surprise, but being told in advance would have been more practical. *Oh well.* I relaxed back into my seat and helped myself to the complimentary bottle of sparkling water in the door compartment.

Anticipation and excitement brewed as we neared the airport. Soon I would be enjoying a romantic night in Jeju with my love. I never dreamed of a birthday gift so special.

I knew we were close when I heard planes flying low overhead. We entered the airport carpark and came to a stop at the drop-off section in front of the departures termi-nal. "Do I need to pay?" I asked awkwardly. A taxi like this wouldn't come cheap.

"No. It has already been taken care of." The driver exited the vehicle and opened the door for me. "Goodnight, Ms. Gibson. Have a pleasant journey."

"Thank you. Goodnight."

Check-in was a painless procedure despite not having the ticket on me. Only my name was required to print the boarding pass. Holding it in my hands made the reality of the situation sink in. "Jeju Island—Departure time: 21:00. Gate 17," read the smooth white slip of paper. I tucked it into my bag.

Stomach rumbling, I ate the chocolate while I waited for my flight, watching planes take off and arrive through the window. I had butterflies in my stomach.

It occurred to me that I had no idea what to do once I arrived at Jeju Island, since I didn't know where I was supposed to meet Jinseung. He wouldn't meet me at the airport—that would be much too public. *Why hasn't he contacted me yet?* I wondered with a sigh. Right on cue, my phone started to ring, Jinseung's name on the screen. *It's about time.*

"*Oppa*?" I answered.

"Please tell me you're at the airport," he said wearily.

"Yes, I am."

"Thank goodness! I was worried since you didn't reply to my message. I've been on set all day and only managed to check my phone just now."

"What message?"

"You didn't get it? Damn. It must not have gone through for some reason. But you got the flowers, right?"

"Flowers?"

"Are you joking?"

"No, I'm not."

I flashed back to the flower bouquet lying on the street outside the apartment building. *Was that meant for me? What happened to it? How strange…*

"Damn. Everything has gone wrong today, hasn't it? At least you made it to the airport."

I decided not to bring up the fate of the flowers. I didn't wish to cause him any more frustration. "What should I do when I get to Jeju?"

"A taxi will meet you and take you to the hotel. I'll let you know what the room number is, and you can collect a key from reception."

"Got it."

"I'm sorry nothing worked out like it was supposed to."

"That's okay. At least I know now."

"I'm going to head to the hotel. See you later tonight. Oh —and happy birthday!"

I smiled at the words I had been longing to hear from him all day. "Thank you. See you tonight."

As I put my phone away, an announcement played over the speaker. "Flight 172 to Jeju Island is now boarding."

———

It was nearly 11:00 pm by the time I arrived at the hotel. My jaw hung agape as I entered the magnificent building. The lobby was huge, with a high ceiling and wide French windows with white frames. Lush green indoor plants contrasted the cream walls. Elegant couples sipped cocktails around small tables, and a pianist played classical music on a grand piano. I felt very out of place and self-conscious in my jeans and hoodie. It felt like everyone was staring at me, wondering what I was doing there.

I picked up the key card for room 73 from reception, as per Jinseung's instructions. My heart pounded as I rode the elevator up to the seventh floor. Once I emerged, I quickly located the room and knocked on the door. I had to make a focused effort to control my breathing and calm myself down. Jinseung opened the door at once. He stood there in jeans and a white t-shirt, his hair slightly mussed, bright eyes absorbing me. "Hey, you. Happy birthday," he said, lips turning upward into a broad grin.

Seeing him again made my heart feel like it was going to burst. I was so overwhelmed that I broke down and wept. Jinseung pulled me inside, straight into his arms. He closed the door behind us. "Shhh…" he said, stroking a large hand through my hair. "Everything is going to be okay. We're together again. I'll look after you."

"Thank you," I spluttered, voice muffled by his chest.

"You've been through a lot while I've been away. Sorry I couldn't be there for you."

"I'm fine, really…"

"No, you're not, and that's okay." He rubbed my back tenderly in a soothing rhythmic motion. "Let it all out."

I sobbed into his broad, hard chest until his t-shirt was damp with my tears.

When I finally stopped crying, I slowly peeled away from the warmth and safety of his muscular arms. "I'm sorry," I said, wiping my wet cheeks. "It's just—"

"No need to apologise," he said, brushing an errant tear from my chin. "Sit down and relax. You must be tired."

I removed my shoes, slid on a pair of slippers, and crossed the spacious hotel room to the sitting area where I slumped into a comfortable armchair. I gazed out the pair of French doors where a balcony overlooked an enormous pool with dazzling blue water. "Too bad I didn't bring a swimsuit," I lamented.

"It's no problem. I'll buy you one tomorrow," Jinseung said. He stood behind me, massaging my shoulders.

"Mmm…that's nice," I said, relaxing into the pleasure of his touch.

"Anything else you need?"

"Yeah, probably. This was all such a big surprise, I didn't think to bring anything with me."

"It wasn't meant to be quite so surprising. If only you got my message…"

"I spent practically all day thinking you'd forgotten my birthday."

Jinseung grimaced. "That's terrible."

"I shouldn't have doubted you."

He shook his head. "I would have thought the same if I were you."

"Never mind. I'm just glad to be here with you."

"Me too. Are you hungry? Have you had dinner?"

"Nope."

"I haven't eaten either. How about I order room service?"

"Sounds good. I'm starving."

We flipped through the menu together and chose what we wanted for our very late dinner.

"I'll call and put the order in," Jinseung said. "You just relax. Would you like something to drink? Would you like to have a bath?"

"Yes and yes."

He chuckled. He poured me a generous glass of wine and I brought it to the bathroom. The room had a Japanese-style design with wooden furniture and marble-tiled walls. A large soaking tub stood by a window overlooking the lush green hillside. I poured a scoop of bath salts into the tub as it filled, infusing the water with a soothing lavender scent and turning it a milky colour.

I undressed and sat on the wooden stool by the bath, washing myself using the provided bucket to scoop up bathwater. After a quick clean, I slowly submerged myself in the tub, my muscles instantly relaxing as the hot water covered my body. Wine glass in hand, I gazed out the window at the starry sky. Life was perfect in that moment. Even after everything I had been through, being with Jinseung was one hundred per cent worth it. I doubted anything could change my mind. Nothing could come between me and Jinseung. Nothing. I lay back my head and sank deeper into the water with a sigh.

Between the heavenly warm bath and the delicious wine, I just about dozed off in the tub, but the mouthwatering smell of dinner brought me to my senses. My stomach growled. I quickly dried off and threw on the fluffy robe hanging from the hook on the door.

Jinseung had already set the table. He pulled out a chair for me. "How was the bath?"

"Wonderful."

"You smell nice." He sniffed the air around me appreciatively.

I was more focused on the smell of the food. My tummy rumbled again.

Jinseung snickered. "All right. Let's eat." He served the food and refilled our wine glasses.

I stabbed gnocchi dripping with sage butter sauce with my fork. It burst with flavour in my mouth.

"So, I've been thinking…" Jinseung said, toying with his chopsticks.

I swallowed my mouthful. "Mmm?"

"After Love in Flames wraps, I might take a bit of a break from acting."

"Fair enough. You worked on two dramas practically back to back. Anyone would need a break after that."

"Yes, but not just because of that. After what happened…I need to think about what's best for you."

I stopped eating, pleased by this announcement, but a little wary about what exactly he meant. "I see. And what do you think that is?"

"I think we should go public with our relationship sooner rather than later."

It wasn't the answer I had been expecting. I was intrigued. "Oh?"

"I know I said one year, but I don't think things can go on like this. I can't give you my full support if we're creeping around in secret."

One immediate problem jumped out at me. "The stalker—"

"Are we going to hide our relationship forever?"

"No. I suppose not. But what about your agency? Won't Mr. Kim frown upon this?"

"He sure will, but ultimately there's little he can do. It's not against my contract to date someone, and he can't keep us apart. He'll just have to deal with it."

"And your fans? They'll hate me if we announce our relationship."

"Yes. That's unavoidable. But there are also the good fans, and they will protect you. And I'll be able to protect you more too. You won't have to be alone. We'll be able to deal with everything together, as a couple."

"Hmmm…I do understand where you're coming from."

"No need to make a rush decision. Let's at least wait until I'm done with this drama. Then we can decide our next step."

"Okay. I'll think about it." I returned to eating my meal. Each buttery bite helped keep me focused on the present moment. I could worry about everything else in the future.

"How's the gnocchi?" Jinseung asked.

"Divine."

"Can I try some?" He leaned in and opened his mouth with a coy look on his face.

I fed him a tender piece of gnocchi.

"Mmmm! Delicious." His eyes rolled back with a look of utter pleasure.

I giggled at the exaggerated expression.

"Try some of this." Jinseung lifted a small piece of fish with his chopsticks.

I received the fish in my mouth and swallowed it down. "Yummy!"

After finishing our mains, we shared a small dessert. I felt downright spoiled. "This is my favourite," I murmured.

"I know you like sweets."

"Perhaps a little too much."

"It's okay to give in to temptation now and then," he said seductively before snatching the last piece of dessert.

I pouted. "No fair."

"Open your mouth."

I obliged and he fed me his spoonful. I ate it with a satisfied sigh. "That was delicious." I leaned back in my chair and stretched.

"Agreed. So…would you like your present now?"

I raised a brow. "Wasn't the trip here my present?"

"That was part one."

"So it's a multi-part present?"

"Exactly." He grinned mischievously.

"Now I'm intrigued."

"Close your eyes."

I did so, curiosity and anticipation welling up inside me. I heard a rustling sound.

"Okay. Open your eyes." He presented me with a gift bag, matte black and slightly velvety to the touch with a thick cord handle. It looked very chic and expensive. "Open it," he urged

I opened the thick paper gift bag. Inside was a small black box tied up with a thin piece of silver-coloured ribbon. I gripped the box, heart thudding. It felt surprisingly weighty and substantial in my hand.

Jinseung watched on in amusement as I struggled with the ribbon, but I eventually managed to undo it. I carefully lifted the lid off the box. Inside was yet another box—unmistakably the kind which houses jewellery. My heartbeat intensified. I had never received jewellery as a gift before, except from my parents. The box made a heavy click as I opened it. The velvet interior housed a delicate white-gold necklace with a small round diamond pendant. The exquisite gift had me lost for words. Eventually I gathered my thoughts enough to express my gratitude. "It's lovely…"

"Shall I put it on you?"

"Yes, please."

He removed the necklace from its box then moved behind me. I felt his soft fingers brush my neck as he pulled my hair aside. He carefully fastened the necklace around my neck. Hands on my shoulders, he turned me around to face him.

"Beautiful," he murmured, appraising me.

I smirked. "Me or the necklace?"

"You." His breathing hitched. He brought his hands up to cradle my face, then bent down and pressed a deep kiss on my lips.

It had been so long that kissing him felt entirely new. His mouth moved against mine in an urgent manner, enticing my lips apart so he could flirt with my tongue. I wrapped my hands around his neck and tilted my head, willing him to kiss me deeper, harder. I desperately wanted more of what I had been denied for so long. Jinseung gladly obliged, his tongue clashing with mine in broad, sensual strokes which made me shivery and weak all over.

Just as our kiss was about to reach a crescendo, he broke away, leaving me panting. "You have no idea how much I've missed this," he growled. His teeth grazed my bottom lip and I let out a strained whimper. From there his lips traversed my jawline and then my neck. He kissed and nipped along the sensitive flesh so lightly that my skin prickled.

Unable to endure the teasing sensations any longer, I yanked him back into a kiss. Jinseung responded with a throaty groan. He lifted me from the chair and pulled me flush with him, grabbing my bare backside under my robe. Through the thin fabric of his t-shirt, I ran my hands over his firm, perfectly sculpted body which tensed wherever I touched. It pleased me to no end to have such an effect on him. We sank into another kiss which quickly became hot and frantic with need.

"Do you want me?" Jinseung asked, his breath hot against my neck.

"Yes," I croaked.

He bent down and scooped me up, hooking his hands under my knees and pulling my legs around his waist. He walked me to the bed and laid me down, my thighs still wrapped tightly around his hips. "Are you tired?" he purred, grinding against me.

"Nope."

"Good. I'm not planning on letting you get much sleep tonight."

26

Needless to say, any lingering doubts about Jinseung's continued attraction to me had completely dissolved by morning. True to his word, he didn't let me sleep at all. We made love until sunrise, then spent several lazy hours entwined in each other's arms, chatting, cuddling, and lightly dozing.

Beams of warm sunlight burst through the window and caressed my bare skin. I gazed at Jinseung's impressive naked form beside me, relishing the thought that only I could see him like this. My eyes trailed down his broad, muscular chest slowly rising and falling with his breath, to his firm, well-defined abs, then the tantalising stretch of skin below his bellybutton which disappeared beneath the duvet draped across his lower body. I snuggled closer, completely enamoured. Jinseung wrapped an arm around me and gently stroked his fingertips up and down my back. The comforting motion almost lulled me to sleep. A sudden thought stopped me from drifting over the edge. I rose up on my elbows. "Jinseung-ah?" I prodded his side.

"What?" he grunted.

"We don't need to check out, do we?" The last time we stayed in a hotel, a perfect morning just like this was ruined by rushing to leave on time.

Jinseung rubbed his eyes. "Oh, shit. What's the time?"

I sprang up onto my butt and stretched towards the bedside table.

Jinseung grabbed my arm. "I'm joking!" He tugged me back down. "I already booked the room for another night. You can stay right up until when you need to leave."

I lightly jabbed his shoulder in mock annoyance. "You had me there. What a relief. I don't feel like going anywhere or doing anything. Just hanging out with you right here." I rested my head on his chest.

"Sounds perfect."

I shut my eyes again and pulled up the duvet.

"What about the swimsuit?" Jinseung asked.

"Hmmm?"

"Didn't you want to have a swim today?"

"Oh. Nah, that's okay. Besides, there's a spa, right? No swimsuit required. I prefer a hot spa over a cold pool any day. Maybe I'll splash out and get a massage too."

"Go for it. Just add it to the bill."

"You're the best!" I held his face in my hands and kissed him on the forehead.

Completely oblivious to the time, I had no idea how long I snoozed, but it was early in the afternoon before I finally rose from bed. Dressed in a pair of the hotel's pyjamas and robe, I made myself a green tea. Jinseung was already up, sitting reading a book on the balcony. I joined him outside. The sun shone bright, but the wind had a cold bite to it. I tightened my robe.

Jinseung lowered his book. "You're finally up. Did you catch up on missed sleep?"

"Yes. I did actually. I feel quite refreshed."

"Sorry for keeping you up last night."

"Ha! You're not sorry for that."

Jinseung smirked. "You're right. I'm not."

"I might head down to the spa soon."

"Okay. Have fun."

When I finished my tea, I took the elevator to the spa on the basement floor. The entrance for males and the entrance for females were situated at opposite ends of the hallway. I made my way to the female spa.

Having visited *Jjimjilbbangs* a few times, I was familiar with the routine of public bathing in Korea. I stripped off in the changing room, shoved my clothes in a locker, showered, then headed to one of the spa pools which was designed to emulate a hot spring, complete with faux rocks and a trickling mini waterfall.

Soaking in the hot water, my thoughts drifted to the conversation with Jinseung the previous night, and his suggestion that we go public with our relationship sooner than planned. I was both excited and nervous by the prospect. Excited that I would finally be able to show off my boyfriend to the world. Scared of all the repercussions.

After my role in Hidden History, it had taken a while to regain my anonymity (well, most of it anyway). Dating Jinseung in public would thrust me back into the limelight.

The breakup ruse would be shattered, and the stalking might start up again. I couldn't rely on the police—their investigation had come to a dead-end as soon as the stalker stopped replying to Yeo Chul's emails.

I wouldn't be able to continue teaching. The students would be too interested in my personal life to take me seriously. Jinseung and I would be able to go out together as a couple, but we'd still need to be wary of the media. Then there was the serious issue of jealous fans and my security.

As I mentally listed all the pros and cons, it became clear to me that deep down I already knew what I wanted to do. I wanted to go public with our relationship, and there was no longer much point in waiting the rest of the year if Jinseung agreed to it. Feeling comfortable with my decision, I lay back and sank deeper into the hot water.

After indulging in the spa pool, the sauna, steam room, and a lengthy back massage, I returned to the hotel room in a completely blissed-out state.

Jinseung lay on the bed with headphones on, nodding his head to the beat of the music with his eyes closed.

"Hey, I'm back," I said, trying to get his attention.

He took his headphones off and looked me up and down. "You're all red."

"The steam makes me flushed."

"It's cute."

I sidled up to him on the bed. "I've been thinking about what you said last night..."

"What did I say?"

"You know. About dating in public."

"Ohhhh that. So tell me, what are you thinking?"

I fiddled with the edge of the duvet. "I would have to quit teaching..."

"Not necessarily."

"Are you serious? Have you worked with teenagers?"

"I see your point. Could you teach children or adults instead?"

"Perhaps, but it still wouldn't be easy. People would come to my class to try and find stuff out about you."

"Ugh. That's true."

"And there's another problem. Some of your fans can be overzealous."

Jinseung sniggered. "That's putting it lightly."

"I'd need some form of protection."

"That goes without saying. Anything else?"

"Apart from that, I don't have any other objections."

"So, if we can sort those things out, you're fine with it?"

I nodded, and he squeezed me tight with a hug.

"What about you?" I asked, extricating myself from his arms. "Are you sure you're ready to face the backlash you're bound to get?"

"I made a promise to you that we would go public in a year. That's only a few months away now. Backlash now or backlash a little bit later? It doesn't make much difference in the long run."

"But you'll be able to cope with it?"

"It's something I've been coming to terms with since I started having feelings for you." He grasped my hands in his. "I'm ready to date you no matter the impact on my career."

Now it was my turn to hug him, and I did it with such force that I fell on top of him.

"Whoa there," Jinseung said, grinning at the compromising position we'd landed in. "You're eager."

Taking advantage of the situation, I snatched a kiss.

"I like where this is going," Jinseung murmured, grabbing my hips.

I pulled back. "Actually, we don't have much time. I need to go to the airport soon—"

"It won't take long." He flipped me over onto my back, pressing himself between my thighs.

———

I knew this moment was coming but it was still gut-wrenching. As we stood by the door exchanging our goodbyes, I wondered how long it would be before I saw Jinseung again.

"Cheer up," he said with a smile. "Didn't you have a nice time with me?"

I lifted my head and summoned some positivity. "I did. Thank you for the wonderful birthday. I couldn't have imagined a better day."

"Have a safe trip back, okay?"

"Thanks."

"Got everything?"

"Yup. Not like I brought much with me anyway."

"The necklace?"

"I'm still wearing it." I pulled it out from under my collar. "I have the box too."

"Okay, good. Hmmm…why don't you take this?" Jinseung grabbed the book he was reading off the table. "I've finished it now. Something to keep you occupied on the plane."

"Good idea. Thank you." I accepted the well-worn paperback and tucked it into my bag. Some light reading material would make the trip go much faster.

"Give me a kiss." Jinseung leaned in and puckered his lips expectantly.

He looked ridiculous, but I obliged. His lips were still warm from all the previous kissing. I savoured the feeling.

"I'll see you again soon," he said, his forehead still pressed to mine.

"As soon as possible?"

"Yes. I promise."

"Then…goodbye."

"Goodbye."

We hugged once more then parted. I took one final glance at him before the door swung closed.

The journey home was a simple ordeal. The novel kept me entertained for the duration of the flight. Even though it was the Korean translation, I didn't have too much difficulty keeping up. I was already familiar with the plot, and I used my phone to translate anything I didn't understand. Before I knew it, the plane was preparing to land at Gimpo Airport.

I arrived at my apartment building just after eight in the evening. When I reached my floor, I knew something was amiss. The door to my apartment wasn't fully closed and the lock hadn't activated. At first, I wondered if I had left it like that, but that thought was quickly superseded by something more sinister. I reached a shaky hand to the handle and cautiously opened the door, heart hammering. My jaw dropped as I witnessed the scene in front of me.

27

Astrangled gasp escaped my throat, eyes widening in shock at the devastation in front of me. My apartment had been completely trashed. Chairs were tipped over. Objects had been pushed off the table. The cupboards were wide open and their contents strewn on the floor. I stood, jaw agape, unable to process what had happened.

Once the initial shock wore off, I dropped to the floor and sobbed. *What's going on? Why did this happen to me?* I was so overwhelmed that I couldn't make sense of anything.

At last, the fog in my brain lifted. *The stalker did this.* The stalker found out about my trip to visit Jinseung and went berserk. *The flower bouquet!* They must have intercepted the delivery, read the message, and overcome with fury, decided to take revenge by trashing my apartment. Convinced of this version of events, I pulled myself off the floor. I cautiously walked through my apartment to check the other rooms. It was much the same story. My bedroom was a mess of clothes and upended furniture. The bathroom floor was littered with bottles and jars pulled out of the cabinet and the mirror had been smashed. I winced at the carnage. It would take forever to clean up and cost a fortune to replace everything that had been broken. Worst of all was the feeling of complete and utter violation. I didn't think I'd ever feel safe in this apartment again.

I carefully made my way back to the living area dodging the scattered items on the floor. Unsure what else to do, I called the one person I knew I could count on no matter what.

Yang Bora answered straight away. "*Unnie?*"

I was so relieved to hear her sweet voice. "Bora-ya…something terrible has happened."

"*Omo*. What happened?"

"Everything's all over the floor!" I blurted, unaware of how nonsensical that sounded.

"Okay. Calm down and explain it to me from the beginning."

I took a deep breath and organised my words into something logical. "I just got home from Jeju Island. My apartment has been broken into. It's a huge mess. I think it was the stalker."

Bora gasped. "Oh my God! Are you okay? Have you called the police?"

"I'm all right, well, all things considered. I haven't called the police yet."

"Okay, first thing's first, call Officer Bae and tell him what happened. While you do that, I'll be on my way."

"You're coming here?"

"I can't leave you there to deal with all this on your own, can I? I'll be there as soon as I can."

"Thank you. You're always there for me," I said, tearing up again.

"It's no problem. Just hold tight, okay? Try not to touch or move anything. I'm sure the police will want everything left as it is."

"Okay, I'll try."

"See you soon."

Knowing Bora was coming over to help me eased my mind considerably. Now onto the next task at hand. I called Officer Bae and anxiously waited for him to pick up. After several rings, I began to think he wouldn't answer, but on what must have been the tenth ring, he finally picked up. "Hello, Officer Bae speaking."

I spoke as slowly and surely as I could manage. "Hello, it's Chloe Gibson."

"What can I do for you, Chloe?"

"Something else has happened."

"I'm listening."

I explained the situation to him, and he promised to come over to look at the scene sometime within the next few hours. I sat on the floor, hugging my knees to my chest as I waited. There was little else I could do without disturbing the crime scene. My thoughts turned to the stalker, seething with rage at the knowledge that I had visited Shin Jinseung. If they were capable of this attack on my apartment, capable of throwing a large and heavy vase at me from a window, what else would they do? I shuddered. Now I knew for certain, this person was incredibly dangerous and I wasn't safe. I prayed that the police would be able to catch them because I didn't know what else I could do to protect myself.

As time passed, I grew increasingly tense. Who would get here first? Bora? Officer Bae? Or perhaps, the stalker. I trembled uncontrollably, my body covered in cold sweat.

When I heard a knock on the door I just about jumped out of my skin. "Hey, it's me," came Bora's muffled voice.

I exhaled in relief and opened the door. She stood in the

doorway silhouetted by the bright light behind her, an angelic glow emanating from her outline.

"My angel!" I exclaimed, hand clutched to my heart. "I'm so glad you're here."

"All right, all right. What are friends for?" She held up a plastic bag full of food containers. "I brought some food. My mum insisted. Hope you're hungry."

"I am! Although I must admit that food has been far from my mind."

Bora stepped into the apartment. As she looked around, the colour drained from her face. "It's even worse than I thought."

"I told you it was bad."

"Now I know why you sounded so distraught. Poor thing, you're shaking." She rubbed my shoulder soothingly.

"I'll be okay, now that you're here."

"Let's eat, shall we?"

We sat on the largest clear patch of carpet we could locate.

"Did you call Officer Bae?" Bora asked as she unpacked the food containers.

"Yes. He's going to come over tonight. I don't know exactly when."

"I'll wait with you until he gets here." She handed me a pair of disposable chopsticks.

"Thanks."

We began to eat from the open containers of rice, kimchi, and bulgogi.

"What were you doing on Jeju Island?" Bora asked, mouth part full. "Visiting Jinseung-ah?"

I nodded. "He flew me there to see him on the night of my birthday."

"How romantic!"

"It was, but I'm regretting it now."

"Do you think the stalker found out, and that's what made them do this?"

"Yes. That's exactly what I think."

I told her about the flowers Jinseung sent me that I never received, and the mangled bouquet I saw outside the building that evening.

"This is getting really serious now," she said. "The police will have to act."

"That's what I'm counting on. I don't know what else I can do. Even if I broke up with Jinseung for real, I doubt that would be enough to stop them now. They're obsessed."

"Maybe the police will be able to find some evidence of their identity this time."

"Yes. Good point."

Bora kept me chatting through the night, lifting my spirits and keeping my mind off the fact that the stalker might come back to my apartment before the police got there. I felt much safer with her.

As another hour passed, my butt began to hurt from sitting on the floor. I shifted onto my knees. Bora let out a yawn and stretched her arms above her head. "It's getting late," she said.

"Perhaps you should go home," I suggested, although I really didn't want her to go.

She shook her head. "No. I won't leave you on your own. I'm staying put right here."

"You have work tomorrow morning."

"I'm used to getting by without much sleep."

"Well, all right then. Thank you." I smiled, relieved with the security of her continued company. "Hopefully the police will get here soon—oh!" A text message came through and I fumbled with my phone trying to check it. "Officer Bae is on his way."

"Thank goodness."

The young police officer arrived shortly with a partner in tow—another young cop, but much shorter and pudgier. He introduced himself as Officer Cha. Officer Cha took some photographs around my apartment while Officer Bae interviewed me in the corridor.

"The door wasn't fully shut when you got home?" he asked, a chunky notepad and ballpoint pen in hand.

I nodded. "You can't tell from a quick glance, but if the door's not shut properly it won't lock. It wasn't locked when I got home."

"Do you remember if you shut it properly when you left?"

"I think so. I've never left it unlocked before. I think someone broke in and left the door like that."

"What makes you say that?"

"There's a trick to closing the door properly. You have to pull it hard until it clicks. Someone who hasn't visited my apartment before wouldn't realise, especially if they were in a hurry to leave."

"Sounds plausible, yet there's no sign of forced entry. If you locked it as you say, then someone could have only entered if they knew the code. Does anyone apart from you know the code?"

I shook my head. "Just me. Oh, and Yang Bora," I motioned to her standing farther down the corridor, leaning against the wall and texting on her phone.

"Did you tell anyone the code?" he asked Bora.

"Of course not," she snapped.

"Then, Chloe, perhaps you wrote it down somewhere."

"Yes. In my diary."

"Could someone have accessed your diary?"

"I keep it in my bag. But I suppose it's possible that someone could have peeked while I left it unattended."

"Do you leave it unattended often?"

"No," I admitted.

"And the code wasn't something that's easy to guess?"

"No, I don't think so. Even I forgot it once."

Officer Bae scribbled something down in his pad before continuing. "Has anything gone missing in your apartment? Could this be a burglary?"

"Not that I've noticed."

"All your valuables are still there?"

"Yes."

"Interesting." He stroked his chin. "So, this isn't a usual break-in, then."

"No. Like I said, I think someone wanted revenge."

"Or it might be possible that you left your door unlocked, and someone who passed by noticed. On the spur of the moment, they decided to have some fun by trashing the apartment."

"But I don't think that's what happened—"

"It is odd that nothing was taken. I'll give you that. The messages, the vase, the break-in…It's a lot to happen in such a short space of time."

"Exactly!"

"Still, we must consider all possibilities." He flipped his notepad closed. "I think I have enough. Officer Cha, how are you getting on?" He poked his head around the doorway.

The chubby officer rose to his feet after examining something on the floor. "I'm just about done here. I'll look for prints then we can wrap things up."

"Prints!" Bora whispered to me excitedly.

I mentally crossed my fingers that he would find something.

"Even if we find prints, we'll only be able to compare them to prints found on the evidence you brought in before,"

Officer Bae explained. "That should tell us if it's the same person, but we won't be any closer to identifying them, since we have no suspects. We'll need to take your prints as well, to rule them out."

Bora and I shared looks of vague disappointment. "At least it would be better than nothing," she said.

The two officers worked together in my apartment while Bora and I waited in the corridor. We were tense with anticipation, praying that the stalker had left sufficient evidence behind to lead to their capture.

"They'll find something," Bora assured me. "They have to."

The officers took their time. I was anxious to know what they had found, but I was glad that they seemed to be doing a thorough job investigating the scene.

Finally, the two cops emerged. "Right, we're done for now," Officer Bae said, removing a pair of rubber gloves.

"Did you find anything?" I asked.

Officer Cha shook his head. "Whoever did this was very careful not to leave any evidence behind."

"Oh…" I hung my head in disappointment.

"Seems it wasn't a spur-of-the-moment incident after all," Bora commented, sly eyes fixed on Officer Bae.

He smiled. "Yes. Seems that way. We'll call in again tomorrow to interview the building staff and your neighbours. In the meantime, if you realise something has gone missing, let me know."

I nodded.

"Stay vigilant. Make sure to change your door code."

The police officers left.

Even though it seemed as though they would conduct a thorough investigation, I couldn't help but feel disappointed. There still wasn't any evidence pointing to the culprit's identity. Meanwhile, they were still out there, capable of harming me.

"I don't think I can sleep in my apartment tonight," I told Bora. "I'm too scared."

"I don't blame you."

28

———

Dear Linda Choi,

I am writing to inform you of my resignation.

I paused, staring at the blinking cursor on my screen. Now that I was typing it out, it felt real. I swallowed a lump in my throat and set my fingers back down on the keys.

My decision to resign had come after a recent call with Jinseung. As expected, he had reacted strongly to the news of the break-in. "I'll quit," he had said, voice shaking with emotion. "I'll quit working on Jeju Island and come back to Seoul for you."

I was stunned. "Really? You'd do that for me?"

"Yes. I would."

But he retracted this assertion later on. "I'll be dropped from the agency and Changsoo will lose his job if I quit now," he explained, having had more time to think it through.

I was disappointed, but I couldn't blame him. No agency would touch him, no director would cast him after quitting partway through a drama over a girl. Then there was

Changsoo who was like an older brother to him. Destroying his own career was one thing, bringing Changsoo down with him was another. Jinseung quitting now for my sake was asking too much, even I believed that. Besides, there was another option.

"Chloe? What are you still doing here?" came a voice behind me. The unmistakable Scottish accent belonged to Jake Mackenzie—another English teacher at the *hagwon*.

Startled, I quickly minimised the window with my resignation letter so he wouldn't see. "I'll head home in a minute."

Jake raised an eyebrow. "Everything okay?"

"Yes. Fine, thank you. What about you? Why are you still at work?"

"I taught an extra class tonight."

"Oh."

"Anyway, I'll be leaving soon. Just grabbing this." He reached for a folder on his desk. "See you tomorrow."

"See you." I exhaled a small sigh of relief as he left the staffroom. I didn't want anyone to learn of my plans to resign. Not yet. I would give it a few more days. If the police caught the stalker soon, I wouldn't need to leave, but if the police failed, Jinseung and I agreed that it would be best for me to return to the UK until my safety in Korea could be guaranteed.

I re-enlarged the Word file, saved it, then got ready to leave. In the days since the break-in, I hadn't been walking around or using public transport, taking taxis door to door instead. I caught one outside the *hagwon* and it took me directly to the underground carpark of Jinseung's apartment building.

Bora and Jina had helped me clean up my apartment, but I was still too scared to sleep there on my own. On Jinseung's advice, I had moved into his apartment for the time being, along with Jina so I wouldn't be on my own. I still didn't feel one hundred per cent safe due to the fact that the stalker had managed to get to Jinseung's apartment once before. On the other hand, a new security system had been installed since then and extra guards were stationed in the building. It certainly felt safer than my own apartment.

"Welcome home," Jina said when I arrived. She was sitting on the couch with the TV on, drinking a beer, feet up on the coffee table.

"Hey. No work tonight?" I asked. Normally her shifts at the cinema didn't finish until midnight or later, and I would stay up until she got home before going to bed as I was too scared to sleep alone in the house.

"Nah, it's my day off. How was the *hagwon*?"

"Fine. Teaching seems to take my mind off everything at least."

Jina muted the television. "Have you heard anything else from the police?"

"Nope. Not a word since the last time I spoke with them."

According to the police, the culprit didn't leave any clues. Security footage showed that they were wearing a hood and surgical mask to hide their identity. But one thing has been revealed. From the body shape of the culprit, the police were almost certain it was a woman.

"That sucks," Jina said. "I thought they would have figured something out by now."

"Apparently not. It's looking more and more likely that I'll have to leave."

"When will you decide?"

"In two or three days perhaps. I'll still need to give notice as well. Can't just leave those kids with no teacher. Hopefully, Linda will find a replacement quickly."

Jina rested her head in her hands and let out a sigh. "I feel so sorry for you and *Dongsaeng*. I never imagined something like this would happen."

"Tell me about it." I walked to the kitchen to look for something to eat.

"There's nothing to eat here. I already checked."

"*Aigoo.*"

"I can run down to the shop if you want. I'm feeling kinda peckish too."

"All right. Thanks."

Jina rose from the couch and got ready to leave. "Back in a minute," she said, slipping on her shoes at the door.

I went to my room to change out of my work clothes and into comfy pyjamas. I was staying in Jinseung's bedroom and Jina used the office as her room. Everything in the modern, masculine bedroom reminded me of Jinseung: the chair where he liked to sit and read, the colourful abstract print on the wall by his favourite local artist, and the bed where I had slept in his arms whenever we had the rare chance to spend the night together. I missed him dearly, but being surrounded by his belongings made me feel close to him.

Thinking it would be nice to wear one of Jinseung's t-shirts, I stepped through to the walk-in wardrobe which sepa-rated the bedroom and en suite bathroom. Clothes hung from a rail along the left side of the wall, and on the right, open shelves displayed shoes and accessories. Below the shelves were several drawers. Jinseung preferred to dress casually when he could—jeans, t-shirt, hoodie, and sneakers, but he still had an extensive wardrobe due to all the events he had to attend, and all the freebie items he received from brands. The drawers stored most of his casual clothing, and he hung up his dressier pieces.

I pulled open a drawer to begin my hunt for a t-shirt. As I rummaged, I quickly forgot my objective and lost myself in admiration of his lovely clothes, running my hand over the fabric and trying to remember if I'd seen him wearing each particular item. When I opened the next drawer, something caught my attention—a picture frame with the picture side facing down. I picked it up and turned it over in my hands. The frame held a photograph of me and Jinseung, his arm around my shoulder and his cheek resting on my head. We were smiling. I remembered that day. Jina had taken the photograph after Jinseung and I watched a film at Cinema Lumiere. I brushed my fingers over the glass to stroke his image. The fact that he had printed and framed this photograph brought happy tears to my eyes. He must have hidden it in the drawer until he could safely display it in his room once our relationship was no longer a secret.

After spending several minutes gazing admiringly at the picture, I reached out to return it to the drawer, but a sudden idea made me stop short. As many K-dramas had taught me, there was often something else hidden in a picture frame: another picture, a note, or some other special document. Curious, I carefully removed the back of the frame. Sure enough, I found a message written on the back of the photograph.

7.11.18

A date with my beautiful girlfriend, Chloe. I am falling in love with her.

Now the tears fell freely down my cheeks as I hugged the picture to my chest. Suddenly, leaving Korea felt like it would be a big mistake.

29

———

"I have some bad news," I said.

Sophie looked at me across the table with wide, round eyes full of concern. "What's wrong?"

"I won't be able to teach you for much longer. I'm leaving Korea."

The news appeared to hit her like a punch to the gut. The colour drained from her face and her mouth gaped.

"You must be surprised," I said. "It's all very sudden, I know."

The police still hadn't caught the stalker, or even come close to revealing her identity. As much as it pained me, I felt I had no other choice. Jinseung agreed too. It was for the best.

"I thought you would stay until the end of the year at least, like most of the foreign teachers do," Sophie stammered. "Why are you leaving? Did something happen?"

So far, I had kept my personal issues under wraps, and I wasn't about to divulge them now. "I have my reasons. It's complicated."

She frowned but had the good sense not to push the subject. "Oh. I see."

"I'm planning to come back! I just don't know when. Everything is up in the air at the moment. If you want, I can try and find another tutor to fill in for me while I'm gone, or we could continue our lessons online. Do you have a good internet connection?"

"It's not the same. I need to do this in person. I can't concentrate properly at home."

"Sure, I get that. Then, another tutor?"

She shook her head. "I only seem to click with you."

"Is that so? Well, you're a smart girl. I'm sure you'll be okay studying on your own, and if you ever need help, you can always contact me."

Sophie relaxed her hunched shoulders. "Thanks. That makes me feel a bit better."

"Sorry for leaving you in the lurch like this."

"It's okay. I'm sure that whatever reason you're leaving, it must be important. I hope you're okay."

I managed a smile. "Yes. I'm okay."

"That's a relief."

Her concern touched me, and I knew I'd miss her while I was gone. Maybe that was inappropriate, but I didn't care. We had advanced beyond a student-teacher relationship—we were friends, and I was completely fine with that.

"Chloe?" Sophie asked, snapping me from my thoughts.

"Hmm?"

"I still owe you money for the last couple of lessons…"

"Oh? I forgot about that. You don't have to pay me right now."

"It's fine. I have the money." She opened her purse and emerged with a fistful of bills. She counted out the correct amount and passed it over.

Taking money from her felt strange, but I accepted it nonetheless. "Thanks." I tucked the cash into my wallet. "This reminds me, there's something I wanted to ask you about—"

I was interrupted by the server behind the counter. "Kim Sungmi," he called.

"I'll get it," Sophie said, rising from her seat.

I glanced at my lesson notes while she went to fetch our order. She returned with an iced tea for me, an americano for herself, and two cupcakes with purple frosting. "This is for you," she said, passing me a cupcake on a small white plate.

"Awww, thanks. Looks yummy." I took a bite and washed it down with a large gulp of iced tea.

Sophie didn't touch hers. She watched me with a faraway look in her eyes.

"Are you okay?" I asked.

She snapped to attention. "Sorry. What were you going to say before?"

"Oh yeah. Hope you don't mind me asking, but were your parents able to pay your overdue fees?"

"Oh, that." Sophie blushed crimson. "I believe it's been sorted."

"That's good. I was so worried that Linda would get debt collectors involved. What a nasty business."

"It was nothing really. My parents are busy people. They just forgot, and all the reminders got sent to the wrong place."

"Yes, I was sure that was the case." I drank more tea then set down the half-empty glass. "Shall we get started on our lesson?"

Sophie nodded and readied her books and pens, arranging them neatly on the table.

"Did you manage to get all the homework done?" I asked.

"Uh-huh."

"Then let's go through that first."

She opened her workbook to the correct page. Red pen in hand, I began to read her first answer.

"What about your timer?" Sophie interrupted.

"Huh? Oh, I completely forgot. It doesn't matter if we go over time today anyway. I want to help you as much as possible before I leave. You don't have anything else planned after this, do you?"

"No."

"Then let's take as much time as we need."

"Okay." She smiled and sipped her coffee.

I returned to marking her homework, discussing what she did right and wrong as I progressed. Partway through, I began to feel a little strange. Tired and foggy-brained. On several occasions, I stumbled with my words, unable to express myself properly. Sometimes I forgot where I was on the page. My mind drifted from the task at hand. I felt dizzy.

"Are you all right?" Sophie asked, brow furrowed.

"Yes. I'm just a bit tired. Not sure why."

"Do you want to take a break?"

"No, that's fine. Let's continue." I forced my heavy eyelids wider open and drank more tea.

We finished reviewing her homework and moved on to the next part of our lesson. I had devised a little activity with flashcards. Each card displayed a word, and Sophie had to think of as many synonyms as possible to earn points. I tried to explain the concept to her, but I couldn't form coherent sentences in either Korean or English. For some reason, I felt drunk.

"You're acting strange," Sophie said. "Are you ill?"

"I'm sorry…don't know…what's wrong."

"Let's end the lesson here. You need to go home."

I didn't argue with her. I really did feel sick and knew we

had to stop. We packed up our things and left the partially consumed food and drinks on the table.

"Come on, I'll walk you out," Sophie said, offering me her arm.

I swayed when I got up from my seat, the room spinning around me. Sophie guided me out onto the street. The cool breeze momentarily brought me to my senses.

"I'm going to hail you a cab, okay?" Sophie said.

Good. I'd be able to get home and rest. *Sleep...I need sleep...*My surroundings began to blur. Next thing I knew I was in the back seat of a taxi and being driven off. I faded quickly, losing consciousness.

30

———

I woke up in a dark room, seated upright and unable to move. Woozy-headed, I struggled frantically against the bonds which restrained me, no idea what was going on. Something in my mouth muffled my cries. A piece of fabric. A gag.

As my eyes adjusted to the dark, I saw my feet were bound with rope, and knew my hands must be tied behind the back of the chair. I was in an unfamiliar room, sparsely furnished. A few posters were taped to the walls, but I couldn't make out what was on them. Just below the ceiling was a single dingy window, a clue that I was in a basement room. An overwhelming sense of panic surged through me. I tried to wriggle my hands free from their binding, but it was too tight. I tried to shuffle forward on the chair, but tipped it over instead, sending me tumbling to the hard floor with a loud smack. I couldn't do anything but squirm and moan in desperation.

Where am I? How did I get here? The last thing I could

remember was arriving at the Booksea café to meet Sophie. Everything after that was a blur.

Footsteps approached.

It dawned on me that the stalker must have brought me here. I started to panic, breath coming in short and sharp gasps, heart pounding on overdrive. Whoever was on the other side of that door meant to harm me, and I was completely defenceless—a writhing heap on the floor.

The door opened and harsh light spilled into the room. I clenched my eyes into slits, pupils stinging.

"You're awake." A silhouetted figure stood in the doorway.

*That voice…*I didn't think I had heard it before, yet there was a hint of familiarity.

She flicked the light on, fully illuminating the room. I clamped my eyes shut, then slowly reopened them, taking her appearance in bit by bit. I couldn't immediately place her, but it hit me soon enough. I tried to deny it, telling myself that it wasn't possible, it couldn't possibly be her. But it was. The girl I knew as Sophie, or Kim Sungmi, stood there, crazed eyes upon me. She looked so different from all the times I had seen her before. The girl I knew must have been fake—an identity designed with a wig, glasses, makeup, contact lenses, and more. The young woman in front of me was the real Sungmi. She had fine, shoulder-length hair, soulless black eyes, and thin lips which curled in a menacing smile. A dark aura surrounded her.

"Surprised, are you?" she drawled. "Yes, it's me, Kim Sungmi, although that's not my real name. Nor am I a high school student. Have the drugs worn off yet?"

I just stared at her in complete and utter disbelief. I had been such a fool. The person I had been searching for had been right in front of me the whole time.

"You must have a lot of questions on your mind right now, like why I went through all that trouble to get close to you, how I could change my appearance so drastically, how I got you here, and what I plan to do with you." She smirked, eyes glinting. "It was I who sent you the messages telling you to break up with Shin Jinseung. I'm sure you've worked that much out at least. The woman you spoke to on the phone who claimed to be my mother was a friend from work. She owed me a favour. The vase—a low-life thug I paid to do the job. I happen to meet a lot of thugs in my line of work. The person who broke into your apartment—that was me. I couldn't resist."

Craning my neck, I saw now that the posters on the walls were pictures of Jinseung. So she really was an obsessed fan.

Sungmi closed in on me. I flinched as she reached out and pulled the chair back up with me on it. "All you had to do was break up with Shin Jinseung and I would have left you alone," she said, stroking my cheek. "But no. You wouldn't listen. You spent a night with him in Jeju. That was the final straw. After that, I knew I couldn't just leave you to roam free." She pulled her hand back then slapped me with such force that I nearly toppled over again. I could feel the blood rush to my face, cheek burning with pain. I could only whimper against the gag.

"You never suspected me. I had gained your trust. You know the saying, right? Keep your friends close and your enemies closer. Kidnapping you was a simple task, really. I drugged your tea. I gave the taxi driver an address near this place. By taking shortcuts and dodging traffic on my scooter, I made it here first and quickly ditched my disguise, changing my appearance enough that the taxi driver wouldn't recognise me when I picked you up. I carried you here. You're heavy, you know that?"

I had absolutely no recollection of any of that happening, yet I knew it to be true.

"By the way," Sungmi continued, "don't expect your wee friends to come looking for you." She pulled something from her pocket—a mobile phone. *My* mobile phone. "I've sent them all a message, saying you took an early flight back to the UK." She twirled the phone in her hands. "This is great, you know. Now I have Shin Jinseung's number and everything. Such fun!"

I twitched with anger, wondering what exactly she intended to do.

"I'm going to undo this so you can speak," Sungmi said, reaching for the fabric tie around my mouth. "I'm sure you have many questions."

I nodded, eager for a chance to regain my voice. She untied the gag, and as soon as I had been released, I let out a loud cry for help. She refastened the tie so tight that it hurt. "You want to die, bitch? I thought you were smart."

Tears of frustration and helplessness rolled down my cheeks. Would she really kill me?

A beeping sound came from another room, catching Sungmi's attention. "Hmmph. I'll be back."

The mouthwatering smell of cooked meat and vegetables drifted in through the door. My stomach rumbled. I needed to eat, and I desperately needed to use the bathroom. Things I couldn't do unless Sungmi released me from my bonds. Perhaps screaming had been rash. Would she dare untie me again now?

She returned to the room shortly, a plate of food in her hands. She pulled up a chair, then proceeded to eat her meal in front of me—a subtle form of torture. My stomach growled audibly. Sungmi smirked. "Hungry, are you? If there's leftovers I'll let you have them, but you'll have to be on your best behaviour."

I watched her eat, praying she would save some food for me. She would have to undo the ties around my mouth and hands to let me eat, which would provide me with another opportunity. But what should I do with that opportunity? Try to escape? Or simply do as I was told and eat, biding my time until a better chance presented itself?

When she had finished, Sungmi took her empty dish away without a word. I waited, tense with anticipation, for her return. I still hadn't made a decision, but my mind was made for me when she reappeared, a plate of leftovers in one hand, a large, gleaming knife in the other. She held the plate beneath my nose, taunting me. "Want some?"

I nodded weakly.

"If you scream again, you're done for. Got it?" Light flashed off the knife blade in her hand.

I nodded again. She set the plate and knife down, and carefully undid the gag. I opened and closed my mouth, exercising the muscles which had become stiff from restraint. I didn't say a word.

Sungmi seemed hesitant about undoing my hands. Perhaps she was still deciding whether to feed me or let me feed myself. Eventually, she unbound them and used the rope to tie my waist to the chair instead. She handed me the plate and a pair of chopsticks. I ate silently. The food tasted bland, but it settled my stomach. Sungmi watched me the entire time, clutching the knife, turning it over in her hands. I bided my time, eating as slowly as possible, trying to formulate some semblance of an escape plan.

"I'm finished," I said at last.

Sungmi retrieved the plate.

"Uh—may I use the bathroom, please?" I asked.

She considered my request for a moment. "All right, but don't even think about trying to escape." She removed the rope from my waist but retied my hands in front of me. Next, she freed my feet. My joints made a clicking sound as I stood up. I took the opportunity to stretch a little. Still clutching the knife, Sungmi directed me to the bathroom. On our way there, I looked around, absorbing as much information about my surroundings as possible. We appeared to be inside a small basement apartment. It was shabby and unkempt, with peeling wallpaper, worn carpet, and a mould problem. The hallway led to a kitchen on the left and a bedroom to the right. The bathroom was near the entryway.

"In there," Sungmi said. She shoved me in and closed the door behind me.

The bathroom was tiny and windowless with a revolting orange colour scheme and a mouldy shower curtain. As I relieved myself, I tried to think calmly about the situation although I trembled uncontrollably. Sungmi didn't seem intent on killing me, or she would have done so by now. She must be plotting something else, I decided. Hopefully, she would leave me alone at some point, then I would try to make an escape. The front door seemed to be the only way out. The windows I had seen were too high and too small. I wondered whether the door needed a key from the inside, and whether there might be a spare one hidden somewhere in the house. In the mirror, I noticed that my necklace was gone. *She must have stolen it from me.*

"Are you done?" Sungmi asked, impatient outside the door.

"Just a minute."

She gave me precisely one minute then opened the door, unable to wait any longer. She yanked me out of the bathroom and guided me away, hand clamped like a vice on my wrist. She sat me back down on the chair and retied me.

"I've got to get ready for work," Sungmi said. "I'll be right back."

I didn't know what the time was, but it seemed to be late at night. I wondered where Sungmi worked that required her to go out at such a time.

I wasn't left wondering for long. It became clear what industry Sungmi worked in when she reentered the room with a face of heavy makeup and wearing a tight mini dress, fishnet stockings, and high boots. "I'm leaving now. Don't try anything stupid while I'm gone," she warned.

I heard a heavy clunk as she locked the door on her way out. This was my chance to escape. Perhaps my only chance.

31

———

I had a trick up my sleeve, literally and figuratively. My bathroom break wasn't just to pee. I had used those precious few minutes to search the drawers and the medicine cabinet, hoping to find something sharp which I could use to cut the rope or as a weapon for self-defence.

"Are you done?" Sungmi had asked from outside the door.

I could tell she was getting impatient. I quickly pulled out the next drawer. That's when I spotted a pair of manicure scissors nestled among the rest of the drawer's contents. *Aha!* I fished them out with my bound hands, and hastily tucked them up my left sleeve. I pushed the drawer shut just as Sungmi opened the door. She didn't seem to notice anything amiss.

Now that Sungmi had left the house, I attempted to retrieve the scissors. With my hands tied behind the back of the chair, the task was a very delicate operation indeed. My constant nervous trembling didn't help either. One false move and the scissors would be on the floor rather than within my grasp. I carefully twisted my wrists until my right hand had access to the bottom of my left sleeve. I strained my fingers trying to grab the scissors, and at last, I managed to catch the edge of the handle and ease them down into my hand. Holding them was awkward, but I was able to slowly hack away at the thick rope.

Progress was much slower than I had hoped, and my hand was beginning to get sore from its awkward grip on the scissors. When my right hand could take no more, I transferred the scissors to my left hand and continued. My aching wrists felt like they were going to sprain, but I couldn't give up now. There were only a few weak strands left holding the rope together. *Just a little more...*I heard a snapping sound and felt the tie around my hands weaken considerably. There was now enough give that I could pull my hands apart, loosening the rest of the rope. Finally, my hands were free. I quickly undid the gag and the tie around my ankles.

I stood up, bones creaking. With no idea when Sungmi would return, I had to act quickly. I ran to the apartment door, praying that I could unlock it from inside. I grabbed the door handle in my sweaty hand and pulled. No luck. I searched the door for some kind of latch or button which would release it but found nothing bar the keyhole. It was no use. The door required a key. I backed away, heart sinking in my chest.

My hopes weren't high for my chance of escaping through a window, but it was my next best option. I checked every window in the house, which didn't take long because there were so few of them. They were all too high and too small. Some were even barred. I crossed that off my list.

With my immediate options of escape dashed, I had no choice but to change tack. I had to search the apartment for either a key, or a means of communicating for help—a phone or a computer.

I checked the kitchen first, thinking a kitchen junk drawer could be a likely place to store a spare set of keys. The kitchen was a shabby room with dated appliances. Several drawers were missing their handles and cabinet doors hung loose on their hinges. The sink was piled high with dirty dishes. I pulled out each drawer in quick succession. Cutlery…utensils…tea towels and oven mitts….*bingo!* A junk drawer. I rummaged through the overflowing drawer searching for a hint of silver or gold metal. My heart leapt when I spotted a likely looking candidate amongst the miscellanea. I snatched it up—a heavy, dull grey key. Holding it tight in my hand, I ran back to the door and tried to insert it in the keyhole. No matter how hard I tried to force it in, it wouldn't fit. It was the wrong key.

I returned to the kitchen, deflated. There were more junk drawers, but no more keys. I couldn't waste more time searching the kitchen. Sungmi could return any minute. I decided to try the bedroom next. The room creeped me out with its Shin Jinseung memorabilia plastering every surface. I approached the cluttered desk and spied a laptop hiding under a stack of papers and magazines. I pushed the clutter aside and opened the laptop. If I could access the internet, I'd be able to send an SOS message. I held my breath as the computer loaded. "Come on…" I muttered. "Please work." A password screen appeared, shattering my hopes. I tried some possible passwords involving "Shin Jinseung" but nothing worked, and after five tries I got locked out.

With every passing minute, I grew more desperate. I searched the room top to bottom in a frenzied state, looking for anything that could help me. Finding nothing but useless junk, I realised I'd have to resort to cruder methods. Desperate times called for desperate measures. At the front door I braced myself, then charged my weight against the door. Even if I couldn't break it down, the noise might attract a neighbour's attention. I rammed myself against the door over and over until my body was aching and bruised. It wouldn't budge. Time for my last resort. "HELP!" I screamed. "HEELLP! I'M TRAPPED." I yelled over and over at the top of my lungs until I had no voice left.

I heard movement outside. There were only two possibilities. Someone coming to my rescue. Or Kim Sungmi.

32

I armed myself with a kitchen knife and waited, tense with apprehension. The clunk of a key being inserted and twisted in the lock was confirmation that Kim Sungmi had arrived home.

I stood next to the kitchen door with my back pressed to the wall, ready to pounce as soon as she entered the room, knife gripped tight in my trembling, sweaty hand. I heard Sungmi walk towards the room she had held me, and her gasp upon seeing that I had escaped my bonds. I held my breath.

"Chloe!" Sungmi yelled. "I know you're in here. Show yourself and I won't punish you!" The floorboards creaked as she moved about the house, checking each room.

Her footsteps approached. Adrenaline pumped through my body as I readied myself to strike. She appeared in the doorway and I immediately lunged at her. My knife pierced the air as she dodged the attack. She knocked the knife from my hand with ease and brought her own knife to my neck. I gulped.

"You've shown me that I can't leave you alone," Sungmi snarled. "I guess that leaves me no choice." She pressed the cold steel blade up against my throat.

"Wait!" I whimpered. 'Please..."

"What?"

"I can give you information about Shin Jinseung. That's what you want, isn't it? That's why you brought me here." It was a shot in the dark, but I had to try to buy more time.

"True. I did want to extract information before getting rid of you. I just didn't realise you'd be so tricky to keep under control."

"I'll tell you everything you want to know."

"How can I trust you after you tried to attack me? You'll do it again as soon as you get the chance. I can't risk it."

"I won't. I can't overpower you. I know that now."

"Hmmm..."

"Wouldn't you like to know more about Shin Jinseung? His most private information?"

I could tell that I was wearing her down. How could an obsessive fan resist such a tantalising offer?

"Sit down." She kept her knife pointed at me as she guided me to the kitchen table. "Keep your hands in front of you where I can see them."

I did so. Sungmi sat opposite me and finally lowered her knife but didn't release it from her grasp. "Go on. Tell me about Shin Jinseung. You better be able to share something good. Something I don't already know."

My plan now: keep Sungmi talking until she got tired. Perhaps then I could have a chance at overpowering her. "Is there anything in particular you would like to know?" I asked.

"Anything that could help me win his heart," she said, completely serious.

I tried to keep a straight face, knowing how ridiculous she sounded. A girl like her could never win his heart, no matter how good she was at presenting a fake version of herself to the world. Nevertheless, I'd have to go along with it. I wasn't good enough at lying to simply make everything up, but I was sure Jinseung wouldn't mind if I shared a few genuine personal details. My life was at stake, after all.

"What does he like in a woman?" Sungmi asked.

"Well…he prefers non-famous women because he desires as much normality as possible in his home life."

"I see."

"He likes someone who is independent. Someone who doesn't need to rely on him."

"Go on."

"I don't think he has a specific type when it comes to looks—he admires beauty in a wide range of forms. Most of all, he cares about personality. Someone who he can share a laugh with, someone who has similar interests."

"And what are his interests?"

I listed everything I could think of. His favourite books, movies, food, bands, games, and more. Even if I didn't know, I tried to make something up. Anything to keep on talking.

Sungmi listened intently but without displaying much enthusiasm. She tapped her fingers on the table impatiently. "I already know most of this. I want to know the *juicy* stuff."

My face reddened, realising I would need to delve deeper if I wanted to maintain her attention over a longer period. Much deeper. I hated to expose such intimate details, but honestly, I had no choice. "Let's see…"

"What does he look like naked?" Sungmi asked, eyes gleaming.

I came up against a wall of inner resistance at the question, but forced through it. I answered in great detail, starting at his chest and proceeding all the way down to his toes. Sungmi was absolutely enthralled, listening with rapt attention, hanging on to every word.

When I ran out of things to say on the subject of Jinse-ung's body, I talked about what it was like to kiss him and described him as a lover. I kept going on, providing detail after painstaking detail, drawn out to fill as much time as possible.

I don't know how much time passed as we talked, but Sungmi was obviously getting sleepy. Her eyelids drooped and she yawned. My gaze darted between her and the knife. *When should I make my move?*

"As much as I'm enjoying listening to your insider knowl-edge, I really must be going to bed," Sungmi said with a yawn.

"I can tell you more when you wake up," I suggested hopefully.

She sniggered. "I don't think so."

"But there's so much more—"

"If I fall asleep, you'll try to escape again, and this time you could succeed."

"I won't—"

"Don't lie to me." She lazily rotated the knife in her hand. "You have two choices. A: cooperate with me and take the drugs I offer you, or B: resist me and you'll meet your end by much more violent means. I suggest you be smart about this and pick option A. It's easiest for both of us."

My eyes were fixed on the knife. *Should I go for it?* No, I decided. It would be far too risky. I needed to distract her somehow…

"Well?" Sungmi snapped. "Make up your mind or I'll do it for you."

"Option A," I spluttered.

"Good. Now get a glass of water." She yanked me from my chair. Knifepoint at my back, she directed me to the sink to fill up a glass. My shaking hands caused water to spill on the floor as I brought the glass to the table. Sungmi produced a vial and poured the contents in, swirling the glass to mix the deadly concoction. Knife aimed at my throat, she pushed the glass towards me. "Drink," she urged.

I wrapped my hand around the glass, heart pounding. "Before I do this, would you answer me something?"

"What is it?"

"Just what are you hoping to achieve by killing me? Do you think you can win Jinseung's heart?"

She smirked. "Tragedy has a way of bringing people together, don't you think? Shin Jinseung will be grieving at the news of your death—so will Kim Sungmi. It's my chance to bond with him. He'll be vulnerable. It's the best chance I'll ever have."

"He won't fall for you."

"That's what you think. Now, drink up."

I trembled violently as I brought the glass's edge to my lips. *This better work...*

Just as Sungmi relaxed her grip on the knife, convinced that I would drink, I threw the glass at her with all the force I could muster. As I had hoped, she dropped the knife on the table. I lunged for it.

Sungmi shrieked with rage. "Now you've done it!"

No time to hesitate, I slashed at her. The knife tore the fabric of her top, but barely grazed her skin. "Give me the door key or I'll kill you," I said, voice shaking.

"You won't kill me. You don't have it in you," she spat.

"Don't underestimate me." I thrust the knife directly at her heart.

Sungmi ducked and launched a devastating kick at my ankles. I came tumbling down. The knife fell from my grasp and went skidding across the floor. Sungmi came down on top of me, pinning me to the ground. I struggled beneath her, but she had me locked down and completely at her mercy. I knew it was game over.

33

———

Sungmi wrapped her clammy hands tight around my neck. "You're dead," she sneered.

I squeezed my eyes shut. *This is it. This is the end.* I didn't pray to God often but felt a strongly compelling need to do so at this moment. *Dear God—my friends, my family, and Shin Jinseung—please make sure they live long and happy lives without me.*

Sungmi increased the pressure on my throat. I couldn't breathe. White spots danced behind my eyelids, and the sound of rushing blood filled my eardrums. My strength was rapidly draining. I was beginning to lose consciousness.

A loud smashing sound ripped through the air and plunged me back to the world of the living, coughing and spluttering. In a moment of confusion, Sungmi had faltered, losing her hold on me just long enough that I could break free. I scrambled to my feet. So did Sungmi. She was first to grab the knife—but it was too late. Police officers in bullet-proof vests stormed inside, guns trained on Sungmi. I recognised one of them—Bae Sangwook. "Drop your weapon!" he yelled.

Sungmi hesitated, but seeing she had no other choice, she released the knife. It clattered to the floor.

"Put your hands up!"

She slowly raised her hands above her head.

At once, Officer Bae descended on her, locking handcuffs around her wrists. "Oh Sejung, you're under arrest. Anything you say can be used against you. You have the right to remain silent."

I watched Sungmi being taken from the scene. I was too overwhelmed to feel relief, my legs like jelly, and my heart pounding so hard I thought my chest would burst. My surroundings became a blur. Figures approached me. "Chloe...Chloe Gibson..." Those were the last words I heard before I fainted.

———

"Chloe..."

"You're okay..."

"It's me..."

"It's safe..."

I heard the fragmented speech of a familiar voice before I came to with a start, gasping for breath. My gaze fixed upon Yang Bora, who leaned over me with a cautiously expectant look on her face, eyes wide beneath her circle-lens glasses.

I grabbed at her sleeve. "What happened? Where am I?" My voice came out in a rasp. It hurt to talk.

Bora stroked my head with her small, warm hand. "Shhhh. Everything's going to be all right."

I had a strange feeling that we were in motion. I heaved myself up onto my elbows and looked around. I was on a stretcher in a small enclosed space surrounded by medical equipment. An ambulance, I realised.

"We'll be at the hospital soon," Bora explained. "Doctors will take care of you, make sure your injuries aren't serious. The police will want to speak with you as well, I'm sure."

One question stood out in my mind, something I couldn't figure out at all. "How did they find me?"

Bora smiled faintly. "I'll explain everything in due time. For now, you just rest."

"Jinseung-ah?"

"He's on his way."

I flopped back down onto the stretcher and relaxed, my heartbeat slowing to an even tempo.

No one was allowed to see me until I had finished being examined, both by doctors and police. My injuries were minor, but it was determined that I should stay in the hospital for a while due to my fragile state.

I was in a private room, small and modern with blue walls, seating for guests, a TV screen opposite the bed, and a small station in the corner for making hot drinks. A humidifier sprayed a fine mist into the air.

For the first time since I had arrived in the hospital, I was left alone. My emotions were too mixed up for me to think properly. Grief for what I had been through. Happiness that I had survived. Terror from vivid flashbacks. Sadness that my life would never be the same again.

A soft knock on the door made me stir. Yang Bora and Shin Jina entered the room. According to the police, it had been thanks to those two that I had been rescued.

"Hey," Jina said gently. "How are you doing?"

"Not too bad." I still couldn't speak much, though the strain on my throat was beginning to dissipate.

The pair came to sit at my bedside. Shin Jina held a large fabric tote bag. "I brought you some essentials," she said. "Magazines, books, pyjamas, skincare products…Everything to make your stay here a bit more comfortable."

"Thank you."

"Is there anything else you need?" Bora asked.

"Not really."

"Jinseung will be here soon."

I tensed at his name. I didn't know how I'd be able to face him after this, or what would become of our relationship. It was all too much for me to process right now.

"Your host parents are also on their way," Bora said, sensing my unease.

"Ah, good." I had listed them as my emergency contact, rather than my real parents back in the UK.

"If you want to rest, just let us know. We can leave," Jina said.

"No," I said abruptly. I couldn't rest properly. Not until I had answers. "Please, tell me. How did you work out what had happened to me? How did you help the police?"

"Are you sure you're ready to listen to this?" Bora asked. "It's a long story."

"I'm ready."

34

Jina made hot drinks at the mini espresso machine in my room while Bora helped me adjust my bed to a more comfortable position. Propped up with pillows and a warm mug in my hand, I was ready to listen to the story of my rescue.

"The first strange thing was the text message," Bora began. "The fact that you would make a rush decision to go back to the UK without even saying goodbye seemed out of character. I called Jina and she agreed with me."

"I saw you earlier in the day," Jina said. "But it didn't seem like you were planning to leave. I was sure you would have told me."

"Yes, I would have," I agreed.

"I tried to call you, but you wouldn't answer," Bora said. "There were a couple more texts from your number—vague reassurances, and then your phone was turned off. Perhaps you had really boarded a plane, but I was suspicious. I thought to go to your apartment—I knew the code since I was there when you changed it after the break-in. It was as I suspected: Everything was still there. If you were going to the UK, surely you would have gone back to your apartment and packed some stuff to take with you. Your suitcase was still in the closet. At that point I knew something was seriously wrong. I called Officer Bae to voice my concerns. He didn't seem worried, but said he'd check with the airport to see if you had really left the country."

"If you hadn't gone to the airport, I could only think of two other reasons why you'd leave the apartment—work or tutoring," Jina explained. "I had been running your errands for you because you were scared to leave the house. I didn't think you'd suddenly decide to go wander out on your own for any other reason."

"That narrowed things down considerably," Bora said. "It was unlikely you had gone to work—unless your class schedule had changed. It seemed more likely that you'd gone to tutor your student. You had mentioned her a few times before—Kim Sungmi. The more I thought about it, the more I suspected her. She was close to you. She could have accessed your bag when you weren't looking. I'm sure she could have worked out your address. However, there were a few things that didn't add up, the vase incident being one of them—she was there with you when it happened. But I realised that she could have had someone working with her."

"You must have wondered why I never suspected her," I said. "I feel like such an idiot."

"Not at all! She was clearly a master manipulator. Anyone would have been fooled."

"Perhaps, but it's so obvious in hindsight."

Bora shook her head. "I still had doubts, it was just all I had to go on."

"So, what happened next?"

"I contacted the *hagwon* to try and get her phone number,

but they wouldn't give it to me. 'It's confidential,' they said."
She rolled her eyes. "In the meantime, Officer Bae came back
to me. He confirmed that you hadn't left Korea. Said he'd try
and track you down. I was feeling suspicious of Kim Sungmi.
I told him as much, but I had no evidence. I didn't know if he
would take it as a serious lead or not. I decided to do my own
investigation with the help of Jina *Unnie*."

"We needed to find out where you were having the
tutoring sessions," Jina explained. "You hadn't mentioned it
to either of us before."

"But *Unnie* remembered something—a detail that seemed
completely insignificant at the time."

"When we met at the cinema you came straight from
tutoring. You were holding a bag from Booksea. I've been
there before and remembered the café. It clicked as a possible
location where you could tutor someone."

"It was a strong enough lead, so we jumped on it. We
didn't have much time. Booksea was about to close. We raced
there to ask the staff if anyone had seen you. They were in the
process of closing up when we arrived—wiping counters and
telling the last patrons to get ready to leave. They tried to turn
us away, but I insisted that we needed to speak to someone
concerning a missing person. That piqued their interest and
we were invited to speak with the manager. I showed him a
photo of you on my phone and asked if you had been there
earlier that day."

"He recognised you straight away! Knew your name and
everything."

"Makes sense," I said. "I had been going there regularly
and I gave my name whenever I ordered."

"I asked if he had noticed anything strange happen," Bora
said. "My hopes weren't high, but to my surprise, he said yes.
Something strange did happen. You left much earlier than

usual. You looked unwell—like you were going to faint. Kim Sungmi led you out of the building. This was the crucial information we had been searching for. I called Officer Bae straight away. He agreed it was suspicious and said he would come to investigate. We stayed there with the manager past closing until Officer Bae arrived.

"From there, things pretty much fell into place. Security footage showed you getting into a taxi and Kim Sungmi leaving on a scooter. The motorcycle helmet fit in with past evidence. Officer Bae got the taxi company to trace where you had gone."

"So that's how you found me…"

"There's more. The police had to work out which house you were in as it wasn't clear based on where the taxi had dropped you off. Officers in plain clothes were dispatched to search the area. They had to be discreet—if Sungmi knew that police were hot on her tail she could have killed you and fled. Luckily it didn't take long to locate you. Screams were heard coming from a basement apartment. That's when Officer Bae and his colleagues got ready to storm inside and arrest Kim Sungmi, or I should say, Oh Sejung."

"How did they work out her name?" I asked.

"It's the name the scooter was registered under, the name on her driver's licence."

Listening to Bora, I hadn't noticed that a fourth person had entered the room. Shin Jinseung stood there in the doorway watching on in silence.

35

Jinseung looked like a ghost—pale-skinned and hollow-eyed. "Please, don't let me disturb you," he said in a faltering voice.

He had obviously been hit hard by the news of my kidnapping. My heart ached for him. "You're not disturbing anything," I said. "Come in."

He hesitantly walked over. Jina and Bora's eyes met, and they nodded at each other. "We'll leave you two alone," Jina said. They scurried away, leaving us in privacy.

A heavy silence engulfed the room. Jinseung fell to his knees at my bedside. He didn't say anything, just burrowed his head in my blanket. His shoulders shook. I realised he was weeping. *"Oppa..."* I said softly, laying a hand on his back.

He lifted his head but avoided my gaze. His cheeks were wet with tears. "I can't believe what you've just been through," he rasped.

"It's a lot to process."

"I could have lost you."

"Yes."

"None of this would have happened if I had paid more attention to you and made sure you were completely safe."

"It's not your fault."

"Not directly, but I played a part. I don't think I'll ever be able to forgive myself."

I didn't push back because part of me really did blame him. He had ignored me when I needed support. He had brushed the seriousness of the threats aside, thinking them nothing more than an occupational hazard. He had failed to take care of me the way a partner should. I silently watched him grieve, unsure what to do or what to say.

Not long ago I had been convinced that I would never break up with Jinseung, no matter what, but now our future was a mystery. Could I realistically stay with him after what happened to me? Being with him was dangerous—more dangerous than I ever imagined. If we stayed together and went public with our relationship, there would be unrelenting media scrutiny. What's worse, there could be others out there just like Oh Sejung—fans who would stop at nothing to keep me away from Jinseung.

I wouldn't be able to continue the independent life I'd been living, doing my own thing while Jinseung disappeared for long periods of time filming. He would have to stay by my side and support me so I could feel safe through my recovery. That meant big changes for him career-wise. Playing second fiddle to his burgeoning acting career would no longer be in the cards. Would he be willing to accept that without resentment? Could I ask so much of him?

My head ached from the painful thoughts swirling in my head. I groaned and groped for the glass of water and paracetamol tablets on the bedside table.

"Are you okay?" Jinseung asked.

"I have a headache." I swallowed a pill with a large gulp of water.

"I'm sorry," he sniffed, wiping his tears with his sleeve. "You have more right to be upset than me. I should be the one comforting you, not the other way around."

"I have cried enough already. I don't think I have any tears left."

"But you must be hurting."

"Of course I am."

"Can I give you a hug?"

I nodded, smiling weakly. Jinseung stood up and leaned over me, then wrapped me up in his arms. I let my body relax against him, revelling in his warmth and his scent. My ear to his chest, I could hear his steadily beating heart. I lost myself in the hug, letting my head empty of all the negative thoughts so I could be content in the moment.

Jinseung stayed holding me for several minutes, stroking my hair, caressing my back, gently kissing my cheek. He seemed afraid to let me go, like I'd drift away and never come back. Perhaps I would.

"I'll stay here with you as long as you want me to," he murmured.

"Thank you, but my host parents will be here soon. They'll take care of me."

"I see. Then, can I wait with you until they get here?"

"Yes, of course." I lay back on my bed with a sigh.

Jinseung took my hand in his. "Chloe...I don't know what you're thinking—about us, I mean...But just so you know, I'll fully support you no matter what you decide to do."

"I haven't decided anything. I need to think things over."

"I understand."

"What about you? What are you thinking?"

He shook his head. "My thoughts don't matter. I will accept whatever you decide."

"I don't know. I just don't know right now."

But I did know one thing for certain. Being with Jinseung wasn't worth the traumatic experience I had been through.

36

I dreaded being discharged from hospital. Leaving would mean having to face the world again. I'd have to look after myself and start making decisions about my life going forward. Big decisions, such as whether I'd continue to live and work in Seoul, and small decisions, like what to wear and what to eat. Both kinds seemed difficult to make right now. I was probably suffering from post-traumatic stress disorder.

My host parents, Mrs. Soo and Mr. Han, sat on the couch in my hospital room. Mrs. Soo was a short, plump woman, with a kind, crinkly face. Her husband was tall and thin, bespectacled and wispy-haired. The old couple rarely left Tongyeong these days, so I greatly appreciated that they came all the way to Seoul to see me.

Mrs. Soo got up and prepared a mug of the herbal tea she had brought for me as a gift. "It promotes mental wellbeing," she explained.

"Ah, just what I need," I joked, managing a faint smile.

As the tea brewed, Mrs. Soo settled herself down next to

me. "Chloe, my husband and I have been thinking a lot about your situation and we have a proposition for you."

"Oh? What is it?"

"If you're not planning to go back to the UK straight away, stay with us in Tongyeong for a while," she implored. "The fresh air will be good for you."

"It's the best place for you to relax and recover," Mr. Han said. "Seoul is not a restful place."

I hadn't considered going to Tongyeong until their suggestion, but the idea certainly had merit. "Would that really be okay?" I asked. I always felt hesitant to impose on them.

"Of course. You are like family to us," Mrs. Soo said. "We want to help you."

My eyes welled up. "That means a lot to me."

"Consider it, okay?"

"You don't have to decide right now, just know that it's on the table," Mr. Han said. "We're not leaving Seoul until you're settled again."

Mrs. Soo offered me the mug of tea. "Here. Hope it's not too hot."

"Thank you."

I mulled over the possibility of going to Tongyeong as I sipped the hot tea. If I accepted their offer I wouldn't have to go back to my apartment. I'd be well looked after. I'd be away from Seoul and the bad memories of what happened here. On the other hand, I wouldn't be able to go to work and serve the rest of my notice. All my stuff was still at my apartment, and there were still repairs that needed to be taken care of. I'd be away from Bora, Jina, and Jinseung, and the rest of my support network in Seoul.

I sighed deeply, rubbing my temples. Staying put was probably the more practical decision, but my heart wanted me to go to Tongyeong, and after all I'd been through, perhaps giving my heart priority wouldn't be such a bad idea. Some time away from Seoul would give me some much-needed headspace. The more I thought about it, the more the decision became clear. "I think I will," I said. "I'll come to Tongyeong."

"That is wonderful news!" Mr. Han said, beaming.

"I'm so glad!" Mrs. Soo said, grasping my hand in hers. "It will do you a world of good, you'll see."

———

I awaited the result of my latest psychiatric evaluation with nervous apprehension—pass or fail? The outcome would determine whether or not I could be discharged from hospital.

Pass, the doctor eventually determined. I was cleared to leave, handed meds for PTSD, and sent on my way. Mr. Han and Mrs. Soo met me at the hospital to drive me directly to their home in Tongyeong. Yang Bora met me as well, wheeling along two large suitcases with her. "I packed as much as I could," she said.

"Thank you for doing this for me," I said. "To be honest, I'd been dreading going back to that apartment. Such a relief that I don't have to."

"It's okay. Besides, the fact that you're letting me stay there for free more than makes up for it!"

Since I wouldn't be living at the apartment but still had to serve the notice period on the contract, I had asked Bora if she wanted to live there in my absence. She had jumped at the chance. The apartment was much closer to her workplace than her current residence, and she had always wanted to live by herself. In exchange, she had tidied up and packed my belongings for me. She would also deal with the repairs which still needed to be taken care of. My insurance would cover the cost. As for my job, Linda Choi had been informed that I wouldn't be able to return to work. She was understanding of my situation. With all of the practicalities taken care of, I felt reassured of my decision to go to Tongyeong. The only loose strand was Shin Jinseung, but it hurt too much to think about. I needed time and space to reflect on that issue.

Mr. Han drove his car from the carpark to the pick-up spot outside the hospital. He hopped out. "Are you all set?"

"Yes, I think so," I replied.

He hauled my luggage into the car boot.

"Have a nice time in Tongyeong," Bora said. "Keep in touch."

"I promise I will," I said, giving her a hug.

I wound the window down and waved to her as Mr. Han drove away from the hospital. Bora waved back, smiling kindly. She had done so much for me. Letting her use the apartment was the least I could do in return, and wouldn't even begin to pay back her unlimited kindness. I watched her until she faded from view then closed the window.

Mr. Han was a slow and cautious driver, and that fact wasn't helped by the small, old car he drove. I had a feeling the journey to Tongyeong would take much longer than it should. Not that I minded too much. Watching the world go by outside the car window soothed me.

Leaving Seoul, the landscape slowly morphed from high-density tall buildings to green countryside, sparsely scattered with small houses. At one point we stopped to eat the lunch boxes Mrs. Soo had packed—yummy *gimbap* with boiled eggs and pickled radish on the side.

Back in the car for the final leg of our journey, Mrs. Soo

nodded off to sleep in the passenger seat. I was growing drowsy too. Long car rides tended to have that effect on me. The rest of the journey passed quickly, and the next time I looked out the window, I realised we had arrived in Tongyeong. The calm, seaside town quietly bustled with locals going about their daily lives. Even with the window closed, I thought I could smell and taste the crisp, salty air.

My host parents lived in an area called Inpyeong-dong—a small neighbourhood near the Gyeongsang National University Tongyeong campus where Mr. Han worked as a professor. We drove up the winding driveway through a large, slightly overgrown section to a ramshackle yet charming cottage.

I took one suitcase, Mr. Han took the other. Returning to this cottage strangely felt like coming home. The interior hadn't changed one bit since I lived there as a teenager, except that the wooden furniture was even more shabby, and the wallpaper more faded. I still recognised the framed family photographs (including some of me), stacks of well-worn books, and sentimental ornaments which dotted the rooms' surfaces.

Mrs. Soo and I drank cold barley tea as a refreshment while Mr. Han went next door to pick up their golden retriever, Snow, who the neighbour had been looking after while they were gone.

As soon as Mr. Han returned, Snow came rushing to me, wagging her tail and panting. She even let out a little bark of joy as I petted her. She got up on the couch with her front paws and licked my face.

"She's missed you." Mr. Han chuckled.

"Good girl," I said, ruffling the sweet dog's soft fur.

After catching up with Snow, I brought my suitcases to the room I would be staying in—Seri's old bedroom. I opened a dresser drawer so I could start putting my clothes away but saw that it was still full of Seri's old things.

"Let me help you," Mrs. Soo said, appearing behind me. "I can move my daughter's stuff to another room."

"Are you sure? I can just keep my things in my suitcases."

"Don't be silly. It's not a hassle. I want you to feel like you're at home." She started removing the items from Seri's drawer.

Once adequate space was made, Mrs. Soo helped me unpack my things away and made up the *yo*, our conversation turned to the subject of my parents. "How are they holding up?" she asked. "They must have been devastated to hear what happened to you."

I squirmed, embarrassed to tell her the truth. "Actually, I still haven't told them."

Her mouth dropped. "*Omo*! You need to tell them. It is a parent's right to know such things."

"I know...but I can just imagine how they'll react. It makes me feel sick."

"I would call on your behalf if I could, but my English is too poor."

"I'll call them. Just not today."

Mrs. Soo fixed me a stern look. "All right, but don't leave it too long."

I wished that I could keep it a secret, yet I knew Mrs. Soo was right. They had to know, and I would have to be the one to have to tell them.

37

The time had come. I couldn't put it off any longer. My parents needed to know the difficult truth: They had almost lost their daughter. My hand trembled as I picked up my phone and opened my contact list. I took a deep breath as I tapped on my mother's name, and before I could talk myself out of it, I pressed the call button.

I held the phone to my ear. My stomach churned as I waited for her to pick up. Secretly I prayed that she wouldn't answer so I could put it off again. But she did answer. "Hello, my dear," she said cheerfully.

"Uh, hi, Mum," I squeaked.

"It's so good to hear your voice. You should call more often."

"Yeah, sorry about that."

"How are you getting on? Everything okay?"

"Um…is Dad there?"

"Yes, he's around somewhere. Do you want to speak to him?"

"I want to speak to both of you. Could you grab him and put the call on speakerphone?"

"Sure. Just a minute."

There was a rustling sound, and I could hear my mother consulting with my father in the background. "It's Chloe… She wants to speak to us…How do you turn the speaker on?…Ugh!"

The call cut out and I knew she must have hung up by accident. She called back a few seconds later. "Sorry about that. Think I've got it working now. Here's Dad."

"Hi, sweetie, how's things?" he asked.

"Actually…" My voice wavered. "I need to tell you something."

My parents were silent for a moment as if contemplating the seriousness of what I was about to tell them. "We're listening," Dad said solemnly.

I came out with the truth of what happened, starting with my kidnapping, then expanding to explain the background series of events which led to it. Telling them was painful. Having to relive the trauma through recounting it and hearing the reaction of my parents made me feel utterly sick to my stomach. I was crying on the phone. My mother was absolutely hysterical and partway through booking the next plane to Seoul before I stopped her. "I'm not in Seoul. I'm in Tongyeong with my host parents. I already have a flight booked back to the UK. I'll come home," I said.

"When will you come?" she asked.

"Later this month."

"That's not soon enough. You need to come home now!"

"I don't have the energy for a long-haul flight right now. I want to relax and rest some more first, but perhaps I could bring the flight forward a bit."

"Yes. Please do. We'll cover any change fees—just do it."

"Okay. I will." Anything to appease her and get her off my case.

As we spoke at length on the phone, she continued to fuss mixed with a healthy dose of victim-blaming for good measure:

"You let yourself go through all that for a boy?"

"Why didn't you just leave Korea?"

"If you told us what was going on, we wouldn't have let this happen to you."

Meanwhile my dad didn't say much, but I knew he must be heartbroken. He was the type to grieve in silence.

After a multitude of "I love yous" and "Take cares," I was finally allowed to hang up. I felt relieved to have gotten the call out of the way, but at the same time anxious and upset about what my parents must be thinking. I drooped down on the couch, exhausted. Snow came sniffing around me. As if sensing something was wrong, she jumped up on the couch and rested her head on my lap—her version of a cuddle. Her presence calmed me considerably. I stroked her head. "Life is so simple for a dog, isn't it? I envy you."

I could have moped around all day but resisted the urge. "How about a walk?" I asked Snow. Some fresh air would do me good.

"Woof!" she replied, getting off my lap and running excitedly to the door.

The sun had yet to rise when we left the house, but soon enough the first rays of light began to burst from the horizon, painting the sky pink and gold. I took Snow for a walk around the neighbourhood, passing many familiar landmarks as we went—the park with the view of the ocean, the walking track, the seaside café. I remembered walking this route with Jinseung the last time I was in Tongyeong. *Jinseung.* My heart stirred and an unbearable sadness washed over me. I hadn't even said goodbye to him.

"Come on, Snow. Let's turn back," I said.

Snow suddenly started going crazy. Yapping and tugging hard on the lead.

"What is it?" I asked.

I followed her to the source of her excitement. I couldn't believe my eyes.

38

I froze, completely stunned. *Am I dreaming? This can't be possible...* Yet there he was. Shin Jinseung. A vision bathed in dappled sunlight. Tall and lean in a thin white button-up shirt and jeans, the wind ruffling his dark hair. His lips parted slightly, intense eyes taking me in. He looked just as shocked to see me as I was to see him.

"Jinseung-ah! What are you doing here?" I stammered.

His shocked appearance wore off, replaced by a fond gaze. "Visiting my parents," he said. "But I must admit I had an ulterior motive. I thought I might see you here. Still, I didn't expect to run into you so early in the morning. I was just taking a walk to clear my head. I'm not prepared."

I opened my mouth to speak but couldn't think of anything to say. I was too stunned. Too mixed up with my emotions. I didn't know how to react to his presence.

His eyes flitted down my throat. "You're wearing the necklace I gave you."

I touched it unconsciously. "I always wear it." Thankfully,

the police returned it to me, along with the other possessions Oh Sejung had taken—my bag, wallet, and phone.

"I'm glad." Smiling, he took a step towards me and placed a gentle hand on my arm. "Well, I guess now's as good a time as any. I know you came here wanting space. Forgive me for the intrusion, but I have to get something off my chest. Will you listen?"

"Yes," I said without hesitation. He had come all the way here to see me. The romance of the gesture wasn't lost on me. I would hear him out.

His grip on my arm tightened. "Chloe..." His voice was soft and low, almost a whisper. "I know I said that my thoughts don't matter, and that's still the case, but I want to express them to you anyway. The truth is, you mean the world to me. I want you to stay. I want you to continue being my girlfriend and I want you to stay here with me."

My heart fluttered at the sincerity of his words. "Really?"

"Yes. That's my wish."

I felt a blush creep onto my cheeks. "Thank you for telling me." Hearing his feelings removed an invisible burden from me. Now I knew where he stood and I could move forward without any confusion.

"If you decide to stay, I'll put all my projects on hold to be by your side until you have fully recovered. I'll buy another house, one with the best security possible, and you can live there with me. I'll make sure you're safe, no matter the cost."

"What about Love in Flames?"

"I've come clean to the director about my relationship with you and what happened. He took pity on me—or perhaps he thought I'd walk out if he didn't accommodate me. Anyway, all non-essential scenes involving my character have been scrapped and the schedule has been reorganised so I can take a little bit of time off. After that...I'm not sure. It will depend on what happens with you and me."

"I see…"

"I won't pressure you, Chloe. Do whatever you think is best."

I looked down at the ground, the hopelessness of the situation heavy on my shoulders. "I can't stay here even if I wanted to. I quit my job. My visa will expire, and I'll be kicked out of the country."

"I'll find a way around that."

"I already have a flight booked. My parents are waiting for me to come home."

"Go home. See your parents. I won't stop you."

"And then?"

"You can come back here when you're ready. I'll wait for you. As long as it takes."

The offer was tempting, I couldn't deny it. But still…there was so much to take into account. "I…I'll think about it."

Jinseung dropped his hand from my arm. "I've said all I had to say. I'm glad I got it off my chest."

"I'm sorry I can't promise you anything."

He smiled faintly. "Don't worry. After everything you've been through, I don't blame you one bit. To put myself in your shoes…I don't know what I'd do."

Snow was beginning to get restless, tugging on the lead and whining.

"I should get going," I said.

Jinseung nodded.

"Come on, Snow."

"Wait." Jinseung reached out again. "Can I hug you?"

I stopped. "What if someone sees?"

"I don't care. Let them see."

Public displays of affection had always been forbidden

territory for us, so his nonchalance took me by surprise, but at the same time I was happy. I opened my arms to him, and he stepped into my embrace. He felt so perfect. Warm and solid and strong. He smelled like a mixture of spice and sea salt. He pulled me closer, one arm wrapped tight around my waist, the other around my shoulders. My head was tucked under his chin. We stayed hugging each other as if it would be our last embrace. Perhaps it would be. He brought his lips down to my ear and said something I wasn't expecting. Three words he had never spoken to me before. "I love you."

39

———

I woke up in my childhood bedroom and for a few minutes it felt like the events of the past year had been a dream. I looked around the room in a daze then reality sank in. Everything really had happened. Starring in a K-drama, dating a famous actor, being stalked, kidnapped, and nearly killed. I groaned and pulled the covers up to my chin.

The artefacts of my childhood surrounded me—books which I had read until the spines cracked, toys I played with as a little kid, photographs of me and my high-school friends, posters of bands I used to enjoy. I lay in the same bed with the floral duvet cover I slept on throughout my teenage years. I didn't feel a pleasant sense of nostalgia. The room didn't comfort me at all. Instead, it felt oddly surreal. Like I was frozen inside a time capsule, but with an eerie sense of detachment—like the items in the room belonged to me in another life.

Ultimately, I had little choice but to leave Korea. My parents would have been unbearably upset if I hadn't come home, not to mention my visa was expiring anyway. And

Jinseung? I asked him to wait for me. Our relationship was on hold until I could decide whether I wanted to stay with him or not. That would depend on whether or not I could get over the trauma of being kidnapped, and my willingness to go back to Korea and put up with the downsides of dating a celebrity—crazy fans and all.

A soft knock startled me from my snooze. My dad pushed the door ajar and popped his head into the room. "Breakfast is ready. I made your favourite."

The smell wafted in—the rich, mouthwatering scent of butter, fresh bread, fried egg, and real maple syrup. That was enough to rouse me. I stumbled out of bed, wrapped myself in a dressing gown, and staggered to the dining room. The table was set with plates piled high with French toast, fresh fruit, strips of fried bacon, and fresh pastries.

"Wow. That looks amazing," I said, snapping out of my morning drowsiness. If there was one thing I missed while I was in Korea, it was a good, hearty western breakfast.

Dad brought in a jug of fresh orange juice. He was wearing a novelty apron which read "King of the kitchen."

"Eat up," he said. "A nice big breakfast will make you feel better."

"Come and take a seat," Mum said, motioning to the empty chair next to her.

I piled up my plate and filled a glass with juice. My first bite of French toast made me sigh with satisfaction.

"How is it?" Dad asked.

"Delicious."

"What are your plans for the day?" Mum asked.

"I don't know. I might just read a book or something."

She frowned. "I know you just got here, but maybe it would be a good idea to discuss some ground rules."

I groaned internally. "Rules?"

"Like doing your part around the house, searching for employment, and becoming independent again. You can't spend all your time wallowing. It's not good for you."

I pushed a piece of toast around my plate, suddenly losing my appetite. "I'm not sure I'm ready to discuss things like that yet."

"Fair enough. But we don't want to make the same mistake as last time, do we?"

"What mistake?"

"The last time you moved back in with us. Your father and I were much too lenient. What was meant to be a temporary safety net turned into months of looking after you."

It was something I didn't want to be reminded of. That was a painful time, made more painful by the lack of unconditional support from my parents. I lowered my knife and fork and pushed my plate aside, then stood up, tears in my eyes. "I'm going to read in my room."

"You've barely eaten," Dad said, concerned.

"I'm not hungry."

"Don't be silly," Mum said. "Sit back down and finish. I'm sorry for what I said. I've spoken too soon."

"I for one don't mind however long it takes for you to recover," Dad said.

Mum glared at him but said nothing.

I hadn't even spent 24 hours home with my parents and there was already tension in the air. I wondered if I had made a mistake coming back.

40

———

The sky was dark in the middle of the afternoon. Flashes of lightning and rumbles of thunder accompanied the rain drumming against the windowpane. The raging storm outside made the therapist's office feel even more warm and cosy than usual. I sat on a plush couch, an overstuffed cushion behind my back, and a soft rug underfoot. My therapist sat on the couch against the opposite wall, a small notepad and pen in hand. A coffee table divided the space between us, a tray of tea and biscuits on top. On the other side of the room, framed certificates decorated the wall behind a large desk, clear apart from a single slim laptop and a phone. A bookcase stuffed with psychology textbooks and self-help paperbacks took up the remaining space.

My therapist, Lisa Keaton, was a woman with long silver hair and glasses, tall and elegant, dressed in a crisp white linen shirt, slim beige pants, and brown leather loafers. She didn't wear any makeup but still looked perfect, wrinkles and all. I fancied the idea of looking like her when I was older.

"What would you like to talk about today?" she asked, in her deep yet soft tone.

"I had another argument with my parents," I said.

"What was it about this time?"

"My mum wanted to introduce me to a friend who might have a job for me, but I turned the opportunity down. I told her that I still wasn't sure if I would stay here or go back to Korea, so there was no point in taking a job right now. She completely lost it. She can't understand why I would even consider going back to Korea—or she thinks I'm using that as an excuse to be lazy."

"And your father?"

"He agrees with her. Thinks I should be focused on re-establishing myself here. In the end, I did go to meet the friend for a job interview, but it only made things worse. No matter how hard I tried, I couldn't muster the energy to fake enthusiasm. The woman could see right through me. She knew I had no interest in the job. She rejected me and that made things awkward between her and my mum. My mum blames me, of course—'you should have put more effort in.'" I mimicked her nagging tone. "She thinks I embarrassed her on purpose to spite her. Called me ungrateful."

Lisa gave me a sympathetic look. "I can see how that situation was difficult for you, but I'm sure your mother thought she was genuinely helping by getting you a job lead."

"I know, but her way of helping is messed up. She puts her interests above mine and completely dismisses my feelings."

"She could have lost you. Does it seem reasonable to you that she might be trying to hold onto you, keep you close to her?"

"I suppose so," I said with a sigh. "But it's not her right to make that decision for me."

"How seriously are you considering going back to Korea?"

"My life, everything I care about, is in Korea."

"But there's something holding you back…"

"I'm not over the trauma of what happened there. I think I'll have flashbacks and panic attacks. I think I'll be paranoid about something similar happening all over again."

"You feel safer here?"

"Yes, I do."

"What if you were just as safe in Korea as you are here?"

"Then it would be a no-brainer. I would go back."

"So, you're left with two options: staying in a bubble of safety or facing your fears."

"When you put it like that it seems obvious that I should face my fears, but how can I when the fear is so paralysing? Meanwhile, I'm stuck in limbo, unable to move forward with my life, testing my parents' patience to the limit."

"Your only reason to stay here is that it feels safe, correct?" I nodded.

"Logic tells us that bad things can happen anywhere," she explained. "One place isn't necessarily safer than another, yet fear overrides this logic. You are not any safer here than in Korea. Your sense of safety is a construct of the mind."

She spoke sense and I understood what she was getting at, but I had a special case. "I told you I was dating someone famous in Korea, right? That made me a target. If I want to keep dating him, there will be other crazy people out to get me. That's what my fear tells me, anyway."

Lisa's face brightened as if she had an epiphany. "Ah, so perhaps it is your relationship that scares you more than the location."

"That could be the case," I admitted.

"It seems like we're getting to the heart of the issue. How interesting."

Another flash of lightning lit up the room. Booming thunder rattled the window frames. The storm matched the tumultuous state of my mind. I sat silent for a while, ruminating.

"Tea?" Lisa offered.

"Yes, please."

She poured me a small cup. A few sips of the soothing chamomile tea and I managed to voice what I was thinking. "I would probably be fine going back to Korea if I broke up with my boyfriend, but I don't want to lose him. I really don't. I love him."

Lisa nodded with understanding. "It's not easy. Your only way to hold onto him is to face your fears. You have to decide whether he's worth it or not."

"I feel completely frozen. My brain tells me one thing, my heart tells me another."

"It's your love and your fear fighting for dominance."

"What can I do?" I looked at her hopefully, wishing she could give me all the answers, but knowing she could not.

"Deep in your heart, you know what you truly want. My advice would be to figure that out, then start taking baby steps to get there."

*What I truly want...*A life with Shin Jinseung and all the positives and negatives that go along with it? Or something else? A regular life with a regular partner? An exciting life with its ups and downs, or a stable, if boring, life? I would need to do a lot of soul searching to come up with the answers, but I didn't have much time. Jinseung wouldn't wait forever. Take too long and I could lose him.

"Have you been using the journal I gave you?" Lisa asked.

"Yes, I have." I kept the thick, softcover notebook on my

bedside table, thinking I'd pick it up when I was in bed and couldn't sleep.

"Try to write an entry every day. It's a good place to reflect. Perhaps you'll find the answers you're looking for."

"Thanks. I'll do that."

Lisa glanced at the clock on the wall. "I'm afraid our time is up."

That went fast. I stood up and grabbed my bag and jacket.

"Will I see you again next week?" Lisa asked, walking to her desk to set her notepad down.

"Yes. I think so."

"Hope you don't get too wet on your way home."

"It's okay. I borrowed Mum's car."

"Then drive safe."

"Thanks. See you next week."

Outside, the rain continued to pour down. The car was parked right by the front of the building, but I feared that even walking the short distance to the car door I'd get drenched.

I waited a few minutes, standing under the eaves of the building, hoping the rain would ease. I checked my phone and saw a new message from Yang Bora. I read it once, then twice, bewildered by what I saw.

41

—————

Bora: I'm going to visit Oh Sejung. Would you like to
join me?

*H*ow can I visit Oh Sejung when she's in Korea and I'm here?
The question baffled me until I called Bora later that
day. She explained that it was possible to set up a video call
and talk with her remotely. *Ah, the wonders of technology.* With
that mystery solved, I still wondered what made her think I
would want to see or talk to Sejung again.

"I just thought that it might help you on your road to
recovery," she said. "You know, it might help you get a sense
of closure or something."

"I'm not sure…" I replied. The thought of seeing Oh
Sejung again, even through a computer screen, made me feel
incredibly anxious. She was the woman who attempted to
murder me, after all.

"You don't have to if you don't want to, but I'm still going
to go," Bora said.

"Why do *you* want to see her?"

"I'm a naturally curious person. I wanted to talk to her to find out more about her motivations and her methods. I find it simply fascinating. You know how much I enjoy true crime documentaries and stuff like that. I'm sorry if that bothers you, though."

I drew a long breath. "I guess I don't mind. It's just weird."

"If you want to join me, let me know soon. I need to book the visit in advance."

I wasn't going to dismiss the option entirely. Perhaps it really would be a positive step to overcoming my fear. "I'll talk to my therapist about it," I said.

"Good idea. Let me know what she says."

After that conversation, I called Lisa Keaton and left a voice message. She got back to me quickly. "It could be good for you, and there's nothing stopping you from leaving the call if you start to feel uncomfortable," she said.

So I gave Bora the go-ahead and a date was set.

We were physically separated by thousands of kilometres, yet I still felt sick to my stomach when I saw Oh Sejung on my laptop screen. She sat in a small, windowless room, empty apart from a table and a few chairs. Yang Bora sat near her at the table, and a police officer stood by the wall, watching on with his arms folded.

The connection wasn't great, so the image was a little grainy, but I could still make out the beady, pitch-black eyes on Sejung's sallow face, framed by limp strands of thin hair. A far cry from the Kim Sungmi I used to know. Her current appearance gave me the creeps—she looked like a character straight out of an Asian horror film.

"I didn't expect to see you again until the trial," Sejung said, a sinister smile upon her lips.

I didn't respond. Bora and I had agreed in advance that she would do the majority of the talking. I didn't have much I wanted to say to her.

"It was my suggestion," Bora said. "I wanted to see you, but I thought I should offer Chloe the opportunity to be involved as well."

Sejung lifted an eyebrow. "And why would *you* wish to see *me*?"'

"Simple curiosity. I want to understand you, and why and how you do the things you do."

"You'll never understand," she sneered.

"I also have a work-related interest in this case. I'm the manager of an actor, and it would be helpful to know more about people like yourself."

"People like me…" she repeated. "You work at KAM, don't you? You used to be on Shin Jinseung's team."

"Yes. How did you know—never mind. I'm here to question you, not the other way around. So I'll start with this: When did you start stalking Shin Jinseung?"

"I don't like the word stalking."

"When did you start *avidly following* him?"

Sejung hesitated. According to Officer Bae, she had already admitted to her offending, but I wondered whether she would be so forthcoming with Bora's questions.

"Well?" Bora pushed.

"I've been a fan since his debut," Sejung said, apparently deciding she would play along. "When I met him in person at a fan meeting, I became addicted to seeing him in real life. It started after that."

Since we had limited time, Bora moved straight onto her

next question. "And how did you learn that Chloe was dating him?"

"I saw Jinseung pick her up in his car. I saw her coming and going from his apartment building. There were rumours online too. I could tell they weren't just friends."

"Why did you start following Chloe?"

"Initially I didn't plan to. Thought I would scare Jinseung into breaking up with her, but then I decided that Chloe would be an easier target. She seemed more vulnerable. Once Shin Jinseung left Seoul, that settled it. I focused all my attention on her."

"I see."

"These questions are boring," Sejung said, crossing her arms and yawning exaggeratedly. "When are you going to ask me something interesting?"

"Then what about how you were able to track Chloe."

Sejung perked up, stimulated by the new question. "A number of means. I've followed her and had her followed. I slipped a tracking device in her bag while she left it unattended—"

This was news to me. "What tracking device?" I interjected, confused.

Sejung laughed. "You still haven't found it? But I suppose that bag has a lot of pockets, and you don't use all of them regularly. I purposely put it in the pocket which looked least used too."

I resolved to check my bag as soon as this meeting was over.

"How were you able to get into Chloe's apartment?" Bora asked.

"Easy peasy. She keeps a diary and has a terrible habit of writing down important private information such as passwords and her door code. I was able to take a peek whenever she left her bag alone—which was quite often. She would leave it in the staffroom at the *hagwon,* or whenever she went to use the bathroom during our tutoring sessions."

I groaned at my stupidity. So much of this could have been avoided if I hadn't been so lax, leaving my bag around and writing things down that I shouldn't have. *I'm never keeping a physical diary again.*

Bora fired her next question at her. "Who threw the vase at Chloe, and how did you arrange it?"

"Paid a guy to do it. I'm not gonna say his name and get him involved. He was just desperate for the cash. I had Chloe walk with me, and the guy was tracking my phone to see when we would pass the building." Sejung smiled brightly as she spoke. She seemed awfully proud of her exploits. "I had only meant to scare her, but I wouldn't have cared if she did get hurt. Maybe that would have been for the best."

Bora winced, the first sign that she was uncomfortable being so close to Oh Sejung, attempted murderer.

"Two minutes," the police officer announced.

She hurried up with her next question. "What exactly were you planning to do after getting rid of Chloe?"

I braced myself, dreading her reply, but Sejung didn't answer. Instead, she turned her attention to me, looking straight down the camera lens. It felt like she was staring directly into my soul. I shivered.

"You know what, Chloe," she said. "You may have gotten away from me, but in the end, I've still won."

"What do you mean?" I asked, voice shaking.

"I succeeded in my goal to tear you away from Shin Jinse-ung, and that's what really matters." Her sneering, derisive tone made my blood boil, and I clenched my hands into fists. Something in me snapped and I no longer felt scared; instead, a fierce burst of determination sparked within me. I wanted to tell her that she hadn't won. That I was still together with Shin Jinseung and there was nothing she could do about it—but the police officer cut in before I could respond. "Okay, time's up."

The video disconnected, the screen turning black. I was still shaking with pent-up fury. *You haven't won. You'll never win.*

Bora had been right that seeing Oh Sejung would help me. It turned out to be the final push I needed. I spoke to Jinseung as soon as I could get hold of him.

42

———

My life had changed completely and irrevocably since the last time I walked through the arrivals gate into terminal one, Incheon Airport. Yet there I was again, rolling a suitcase over the polished floor towards the crowd of waiting loved ones, under vastly different circumstances than before. I was a little anxious. Bad memories resurfaced about the job scam, and how lost and scared I had been on that first day in Seoul. I reminded myself that was in the past and everything was going to be okay this time. *Deep breaths.*

It had been three months since I announced to Jinseung that I wanted to go back to Korea and continue my relationship with him. Three months of planning, applying for a visa, and waiting for my application to get processed. I had used the time to physically and mentally prepare for my return. Jinseung had also been productive, getting everything in order and communicating his plans with his agency. He had sold his apartment and bought a new house where we would reside away from the city, away from the landmarks of my trauma.

I scanned the faces in the crowd and saw Bong Changsoo. He looked the same as always, tall and pudgy, wearing jeans and a striped shirt. Jinseung had sent him to pick me up since he couldn't meet me himself for obvious reasons—getting mobbed by people who recognised him being the main one.

Despite our tenuous relationship, I was glad to see Changsoo's chubby, unshaven face, and he seemed glad to see me too. He gave me a small wave, and I approached him.

"Hey, Chloe," he said, smiling. "You made it."

"Yup. I'm here. Hopefully for the long term."

"How was the flight?"

"It was great!" I never usually said that about a flight, but Jinseung had insisted on buying me a business-class ticket. I spent the flight in comfort, watching movies and napping interchangeably.

He grabbed the handle of my suitcase. "Let me take that for you."

We headed towards the exit.

"Are you tired?" Changsoo asked.

"Not too bad since I managed to sleep on the plane."

"Ah, that's good."

"How's Jinseung?"

"He'll be so glad to see you. He hasn't been the same man since you left."

A pang of regret hit me. The time apart must have been hard on him. I had been so focused on my own recovery that I had neglected him. I resolved to make up for everything I had put him through.

"I heard that there's going to be a cast reunion for Hidden History," Changsoo said. "Are you going to go?"

"Of course! I wouldn't miss it." An email about it had come through several days ago, and I was so happy that my flight arrived in time for me to attend. I looked forward to catching up with all the actors I had worked with, especially Baek Yena.

Changsoo led me through the massive carpark and located his car among the sea of vehicles. I recognised the black SUV at once. It was Jinseung's car, not Changsoo's. He advised me to sit in the back seat. I wondered why I couldn't sit in the front. Then I opened the door and jumped with shock. There was Jinseung. He had a wide grin plastered on his face, eyes shining brightly below his unruly head of hair. Every cell in my body lit up in his presence. I stared at him, wide-eyed. Seeing him again felt more wonderful than I ever imagined.

"Surprised to see me?" he asked teasingly.

"Jinseung-ah!" I cried, launching myself into his arms. "I wasn't expecting you to come."

"Why wouldn't I? I've been looking forward to this moment for so long. You're finally here!"

I basked in the glorious feeling of his strong arms around me. He stroked my hair and kissed my forehead. "Thank you," he said softly, breath warm against my ear.

"For what?"

"For coming back. For choosing me."

"Thank you for waiting. I'm sorry I took so long."

"You're here now. That's all that matters." He released me from the hug so I could put my seatbelt on.

We couldn't stop looking at each other and grinning as Changsoo drove us away.

"Excited to see my—*our* new place?" Jinseung asked.

"Yes! I've been dying to see it."

He had sent me photos of the house, but I couldn't wait to see it in person. *Our house.* I sat on the edge of my seat the entire trip, barely containing my excitement.

We eventually arrived in an upmarket suburb just out of

Seoul. Large, standalone houses with high fences lined the perfectly maintained streets.

"It's on this road," Jinseung said.

Curiosity piqued, I looked out the window, wondering which house was ours.

Changsoo finally turned down a driveway. He used a little remote control to open the tall gate blocking the entrance. It swung open automatically. The house came into view. Not overly huge. Simple and modern with sharp angles and large windows with dark grey frames on a white facade. Tall trees surrounded the edges of the section, providing tons of privacy.

"What do you think?" Jinseung asked.

"It looks fantastic."

"Just wait till you see inside."

When we got out of the car, I heard a yapping sound from nearby. "Is that…?"

A cute white dog came running towards us, tail wagging furiously.

"Oh! Buster!" I said and bent down to pet him when he stopped at my ankles and pawed at my shoes.

"Since I have the space now, I brought him back from Tongyeong. He's going to live with me now."

"Weren't your parents disappointed?"

"Yeah, but he is my dog after all. My parents are getting a new dog and they're pretty excited about it."

"So, I'll be living with Buster too…"

"Is that all right? I wanted it to be a surprise."

"It's great! I love dogs. This is wonderful." I hadn't had my own pet since I was a kid, so I was bursting with joy at this revelation.

"I'll leave you two—*three* to get settled," Changsoo announced, watching on with a grin.

We thanked him and said goodbye. He swapped over to his own car and drove away. Jinseung took my hand and we walked to the front door together, Buster hot on our heels. He pointed out the security features—an intercom, camera, and alarm. The door was heavy and required a special key that was difficult to copy. The systems in place helped put my mind at ease. I was glad Jinseung had taken this into consideration when choosing the property.

The door unlocked with a clunk. Once inside, I looked around in awe at the place I would call my home. Spacious and light-filled, with walls in neutral tones and squishy new carpet underfoot. There wasn't much in the way of furniture, but I could visualise how it would look with a few tables and shelves, and with art and photographs on the walls.

"I haven't done much to it yet," Jinseung explained. "I thought you would want to help decorate. Make it your own."

"Yes, I would love to." I liked Jinseung's taste in design, but being able to inject some of my own style would make the house much more comfortable.

Jinseung took me on a tour of the rest of the rooms—three bedrooms, three bathrooms, a home office, living and dining area, and kitchen. I had never lived in such a nice place before. I wandered from room to room, the reality still sinking in.

Once my new house excitement began to subside, Jinseung and I settled down in the living room with drinks and snacks to chat and catch up. Buster lay quietly on the rug by our feet.

Jinseung wrapped an arm around me, and the conversation turned from lighthearted banter to something deeper. "You never told me before," he said. "What made you decide to come back?"

I rested my head on his shoulder and sighed.

"You don't have to tell me if you don't want to," he said.

"It's okay. I owe you an explanation."

"No, you don't."

"Well, I want to be honest with you. I want you to know everything."

"Okay. So tell me."

"Part of it was Oh Sejung," I explained. "Even though she's locked up, she looked so smug and happy with herself. Told me that she had succeeded in tearing us apart, and therefore she had won. I was furious."

An angry vein throbbed in Jinseung's forehead. "The nerve of her."

"Right? But I realised that, in a weird way, she was right. If I gave up on our relationship, I was letting her win, and I couldn't stand that thought. So that's one reason."

"And something else?"

"Something that Yang Bora said. She told me that I had made it through the worst thing possible, and that I'd be able to survive anything now. That made me think, why quit now? There will be more hurdles in the future, but I've already made it through the worst part. Things should be much easier from here on out."

Jinseung nodded, a look of understanding on his face. "I get it. Rather than letting yourself be defeated by what happened, you're choosing to become stronger and better equipped to fight the challenges in your future."

"That's a good way of looking at it." I snuggled closer to him. "But I can't deny that a little voice is still there, telling me that I could get hurt again, and making me want to run away and hide. I have to confront that voice every day and put it out of my mind."

"It must be difficult. Will you keep going to therapy?"

"Yes. I'll probably need it for a very long time. Hope I can find a good therapist here."

"Whatever I can do to support you, let me know." He kissed my hand.

I smiled, relieved to be back with him. Everything I had been worried about had melted away, leaving me with a feeling of contentment.

"There's one thing I think we should talk about," Jinseung said, voice turning grave.

My stomach tightened. I already knew what he was going to say, but I still felt wary.

"Word will spread quickly now that we're living together," he continued. "We'll need to come clean about our relationship soon."

We had already discussed this but still hadn't put an exact date on it. "When were you thinking?" I asked.

"As soon as possible. The Hidden History cast reunion is in two days. I thought we could announce it there."

I put on a brave face and nodded. "Good idea."

"So you agree? Are you sure you're ready?"

"I'm ready."

As ready as I'll ever be.

43

Tonight is the night. As I stood in front of the bathroom mirror doing my makeup, all I could think about was how my life was about to be plunged into complete and utter mayhem. My hand shook so much that I messed up my eyeliner and had to wipe it off and start over. I was a bundle of nervous energy pumped full of adrenaline. *I won't back out now,* I told myself, determined to face the night ahead with confidence and composure.

We were about to embark on our first official appearance as a couple. From this point on, the cat would be out of the bag. KAM Entertainment had already prepared a statement confirming our relationship to be released as soon as word started to spread.

"Are you nearly ready?" Jinseung called from another room. "The taxi is here."

I quickly finished blotting my lipstick, flung on my coat, and grabbed my purse before meeting him at the door. He eyed me appreciatively. "You look stunning."

I blushed. "Thanks. You look good too. Is that a new shirt?"

He looked down at the rose-coloured shirt he wore tucked into straight black jeans. He looked hot, as usual. "Yeah. You like it?"

"It suits you."

He burst into a smile and grabbed my hand. "Come on. Let's not leave the driver waiting." We walked out to the car.

Stars glittered in the dark sky, soon to be replaced by the bright, multi-coloured lights of central Seoul.

"How are you feeling?" Jinseung asked during the ride.

I ran my hands up and down the top of my legs. "Nervous, excited, kinda nauseous."

He grimaced. "Better not drink too much then. Don't want you to be sick or something."

"I won't."

He rubbed my shoulder. "Just relax and have fun tonight. I don't think anyone's going to be gossiping about us straight away. Most likely nothing much will change—at least for a while."

"You're probably right." I sighed, letting out some of my pent-up tension. "I don't expect the other actors will spread gossip. The staff, though—"

"Yeah. One of them could leak it, but it's going to be okay if that happens. That's exactly what we're prepared for. Bit by bit, we want the secret to come out. That's the whole point."

"True. I guess I'm overthinking things."

For the longest time, I wanted so badly to reveal our secret to the world. Then the kidnapping happened and changed everything. I still wanted to go through with it, but I felt much more hesitant. I reminded myself that I chose to be with Jinseung, and keeping our relationship a secret forever wasn't an option.

We arrived at the restaurant—a trendy little bistro in Apgujeong-dong. A sign on the door read, "Private function". A velvet rope cordoned off the entrance and a guard stood outside.

Heads turned and eyes landed on us when we entered. I recognised the faces of my old costars—Cho Dongjoo and Kim Jaehyun, who played middle-aged residents of the fictional town in Hidden History, Baek Yena, the lead female who played a detective, and several others who played roles as police officers and townspeople. Yena called us over to the table with a grin and shuffled over so there was room to sit beside her. I reminded myself that she was one of the tiny few who already knew Jinseung and I were dating.

"You made it! I was beginning to think you wouldn't come." She poured us each a glass of soju.

"It's called being fashionably late," Jinseung quipped.

"A traffic jam made us late, that's all," I explained.

Kim Jaehyun eyed us suspiciously. "Did you two come together?"

"Yes, we did," Jinseung replied without skipping a beat.

"So you're still in touch with each other then? And very friendly by the looks of it."

Yena scoffed involuntarily. Jaehyun turned to her and raised an eyebrow. She pretended to cough.

"We're actually dating," Jinseung said casually.

He said it before I could even brace myself. A random silence in the room fell just in time for the words to leave his mouth, and now they hung heavily in the quiet air. It seemed like everyone in the restaurant could have heard him.

Yena gasped, bringing a hand to her mouth. "*Omo!*"

"You can drop the act," Jinseung said. "She already knows," he explained to the others at the table.

"How long has this been going on then?" Dongjoo asked with an amused grin.

"Must be over a year now," Yena said. "So it's no longer a secret, I gather."

I nodded. "No longer a secret as of tonight, actually."

Dongjoo slapped Jinseung on the back. "Congrats, man. Wonderful news."

Jaehyun pouted. "It's a pity. I had been looking forward to this evening because I was planning to make my move on Chloe."

"You perv!" Yena shot back.

Jaehyun chuckled. His dirty old man schtick never failed to rile her. "Only teasing," he said to me with a wink.

"This deserves a toast, don't you think?" Yena said. She lifted her glass. "To the first official Hidden History couple!"

Everyone raised their glasses and cheered. I cracked a smile at their enthusiasm while Jinseung beamed and blushed beside me. With step one of our "go public with our relationship" scheme complete, I indulged in a shot of soju. The alcohol soothed my jitteriness and I stopped worrying so much about the future.

We fielded questions for a while, but eventually, everyone's attention moved from us and onto other people present, catching up with each other, chatting about their families and their work.

During a brief moment we weren't occupied in a conversation with other attendees, Jinseung put an arm around me. "This is nice, isn't it? Not having to hide."

I was about to express my agreement when something caught my eye—a sudden flash of bright light. "What was that?" I asked.

"What?" he looked around, bemused. He obviously

hadn't noticed, but a few others had. A group went to the window to investigate. More flashes quickly followed.

"Paparazzi," someone said. "They've located us."

Jinseung and I exchanged meaningful looks.

The security guard went outside to try and shoo the paps away. They were resistant at first, but after a while he succeeded in getting them to leave.

"They'll be back," Jinseung said. "As soon as people start to leave, I'm sure they'll swoop in to get their photographs."

"What should we do?" I asked.

He locked eyes with me. "Let's take this opportunity."

I swallowed the lump in my throat then nodded.

———

Jinseung was right. The paparazzi did come back as the event came to an end and the guests began to exit. The guard had given up trying to get rid of them and shifted his focus to escorting everyone safely from the restaurant into taxis.

"So, you're okay with this?" Jinseung asked again as we prepared to leave.

I nodded. "Yes. Let's do it."

Before I could change my mind, Jinseung took my hand and we walked out of the restaurant together. We faced a barrage of camera flashes. The security guard tried to get us to move on, but we purposefully lingered, letting the photographers get all the snaps they wanted as we held hands. To make the message even clearer, Jinseung kissed me. It took me by surprise, but I went with it, closing my eyes as he pressed his lips to mine. My heart pounded throughout our display and didn't slow down until we were safe inside a taxi.

We looked at each other and grinned sheepishly before bursting into laughter.

"It's going to be fun to read the news tomorrow," Jinseung said, wiping his eyes.

"Fun? That's one way of putting it."

"Not having regrets, are you?"

I shook my head. "You?"

"No. Absolutely not."

"Good, because there's no way we can turn back now."

"I wouldn't want to. I love you, Chloe Gibson, and I want the world to know it."

"I love you too."

He reached over and kissed me again.

GLOSSARY

-nim — An honorific used when addressing someone by their profession

-ssi — A polite title used when addressing someone

-ah/-ya — A casual title used when addressing someone

Aigoo — An exclamation expressing surprise or exasperation

Ajumma — A middle-aged woman

Ajussi — A middle-aged man

Dongsaeng — Younger sibling/friend

Gimbap — Korean seaweed and rice roll

Hagwon — Cram school

Halmoni — Grandma

Hanbok — A traditional Korean dress

Hanok — A traditional Korean house

Jjimjilbbang — Bathhouse/sauna

Noona — Used by males to address older sisters or older female friends

Oeguk saram — foreigner

Omo — An expression of shock or surprise

Oppa — Used by females to address their older brother, older male friends, or boyfriend

Pojangmacha — A street food stall in a tent

Pororo — The name of a kids' cartoon with a penguin character called Pororo

Sasaeng fan — An obsessive fan

Seonbae — Used to address your senior at school or work

Sundae — Blood sausage

Tteokbokki — A dish of rice cakes in a spicy sauce

Unnie — Used by females to address their older sisters or older female friends

Yeoboseyo — Used when you answer the phone

Yo — Traditional Korean mattress